Book Eight

EPIC ZERO 8

Tales of a Colossal Boy Blunder

By

R.L. Ullman

But That's
Another Story...
Press

Cover design and character illustrations by Yusup Mediyan.

Published by But That's Another Story... Press
Ridgefield, CT

Printed in the United States of America.

First Printing, 2021.

ISBN: 978-1-953713-04-9
Library of Congress Control Number: 2021900081

For Olivia and Alex,
the dynamic duo

BOOKS BY R.L. ULLMAN

EPIC ZERO SERIES

EPIC ZERO:
Tales of a Not-So-Super 6th Grader

EPIC ZERO 2:
Tales of a Pathetic Power Failure

EPIC ZERO 3:
Tales of a Super Lame Last Hope

EPIC ZERO 4:
Tales of a Total Waste of Time

EPIC ZERO 5:
Tales of an Unlikely Kid Outlaw

EPIC ZERO 6:
Tales of a Major Meta Disaster

EPIC ZERO 7:
Tales of a Long Lost Leader

EPIC ZERO 8:
Tales of a Colossal Boy Blunder

MONSTER PROBLEMS SERIES

MONSTER PROBLEMS:
Vampire Misfire

MONSTER PROBLEMS 2:
Down for the Count

MONSTER PROBLEMS 3:
Prince of Dorkness

TABLE OF CONTENTS

ONE

I HATE CARNIVAL GAMES

This is taking way longer than I expected.

I mean, we've been weaving through crowds at the Keystone City carnival for over an hour hunting for Gigantox, a transparent Meta 2 villain filled with toxic growth chemicals. He kind of sticks out in a crowd so I figured we would've found him by now, but I'm starting to think we're looking for a needle in a haystack. Of course, it doesn't help that some of us are focused on entirely the wrong things.

"Is that guy selling corn dogs?" Pinball asks, inhaling deeply. "Yum, I love corn dogs. Can't you just smell that golden-brown, cornmeal batter deliciousness?"

"Keep your saucer-sized eyes on the prize," Night Owl says. "We're here to find Gigantox, not disgusting carnival food. So, stay alert."

"Carnival food is not disgusting," Pinball huffs. "In fact, if I were running the Department of Health I'd make carnival food one of the five major food groups. You know, right up there with bread, fruit, meat, and vegetables. Ooooh, are those deep-fried peanut butter-stuffed pickles?"

"Pinball, please," Selfie says. "Can't you focus on finding Gigantox and not the food?"

"Sure can," Pinball says, holding his stomach. "But after we catch him let's grab a few of those funnel cake cheeseburgers."

Well, Pinball may be as useless as ever, but even I have to admit that staying focused is pretty difficult right now. Between the throngs of people, flashing carnival lights, and fast-moving rides, my senses are on overload. But despite all of the distractions, I need to set a good example as the leader of Next Gen because this mission is critical for a bunch of reasons.

Gigantox is not only a major safety threat, but he's also our chance for redemption. That's because we still haven't gelled as a team, and our last outing at the Keystone City Museum was a complete disaster. If it weren't for the Freedom Force, Lunatick would have escaped scot-free. So, this is our chance to prove we've gotten our act together.

Especially since the Freedom Force is watching.

Now don't get me wrong, I'm thrilled my parents

and the rest of the gang are mentoring us, but it's also a double-edged sword. We're getting the best Meta training in the world, but we also have to show that we're applying it in the real world.

And that's the part that worries me.

"Okay, boss-man," Skunk Girl says, "where is this bad guy already? You said we couldn't miss him about ten minutes ago, which was twenty minutes after my feet started hurting."

"Don't worry," I say, mustering as much confidence as I can, "he's here somewhere." But truthfully, I'm getting nervous. I mean, where did Gigantox go? It's not like he blends easily into a crowd. After all, he's an android shaped like a man, but his skin is made of a clear, indestructible plastic containing a toxic mix of growth chemicals.

You'd think he'd stand out like a sore thumb.

"Um, guys," Pinball says, stopping suddenly.

"Keep walking, Pinball," Skunk Girl says. "I don't want to hear about your love for panini-pressed bacon doughnuts again."

"Um, this isn't about bacon doughnuts," Pinball says. "Look at that guy over there by the ring toss booth. The guy with the hat and trench coat. It's, like, ninety degrees out. Why would anybody be wearing a trench coat on a hot day like this?"

A trench coat?

Just then, the crowd in front of us parts, and I see

the back of a large man wearing a tan hat and matching trench coat. And when the man turns around, I'm staring right through his plastic face at a cluster of metal gears immersed in a bubbling, purplish liquid.

It's him! It's Gigantox!

"Next Gen—Power Up!" I yell.

"Still working on that battle cry, huh?" Skunk Girl says, patting my shoulder. "Sad."

I didn't think it was that bad but I'll work on it later. Right now, we've got a job to do! Our first order of business is to get these people to safety, and as team leader, it's my job to call the right play.

"Initiate crowd control!" I yell.

"On it!" Night Owl yells back as she jumps on a shadow slide and creates a shadow barrier to block the now confused crowd from Gigantox.

"Everyone, please look over here!" Selfie belts out, using her magic phone to amplify her voice a hundred decibels.

Then, I shield my eyes as a white flash radiates from her phone, blanketing the crowd. And when I look back over everyone has been hypnotized.

"Please leave the premises in a quick and orderly manner!" Selfie commands.

"I'll generate a bad odor to corral them towards the exit," Skunk Girl says, generating a wall of stink.

As the crowd holds their noses and starts to move, I have to say I'm feeling pretty good about our teamwork.

Now we just have to apprehend the bad guy. But apparently, Gigantox has other ideas.

"Look out!" Pinball yells.

The next thing I know, Gigantox rips through his trench coat as his body starts growing rapidly! I crane my neck as he grows twenty feet tall, and then forty feet tall, and then one hundred feet tall! And that's when I see something up high that makes my stomach sink.

There are people on the Ferris wheel!

We forgot about the people on the Ferris wheel!

Just. Freaking. Wonderful.

Then, Gigantox notices the Ferris wheel himself and the passengers scream. We have to save them!

"Epic Zero, negate his power!" Night Owl yells.

"Right!" I answer. I concentrate hard and bathe Gigantox with my negation power but nothing happens! Are you kidding me? I know my powers don't work on robots, but does it have to include androids too? And now Gigantox is extending his massive mitt towards the Ferris wheel! I might not be able to do anything, but maybe the others can!

"Pinball! Night Owl!" I yell at the top of my lungs. "Execute the slingshot maneuver!"

"Yes, sir!" Pinball says, inflating his body and bouncing over to Night Owl.

Night Owl creates a long, thin shadow and wraps it around two lampposts. Then, Pinball leans back into it, pulling the shadow taut like a slingshot.

"You know," Pinball says nervously. "The one time we tried this I missed the practice target by miles and had to take a bus back to the Hangout."

"Here's the deal," Night Owl says. "If you knock Gigantox out with one blow, I'll buy you all the funnel cake cheeseburgers you can eat."

"Seriously?" Pinball says, narrowing his eyes with determination. "Then consider me locked and looooaaaadddedddd!"

Suddenly, Pinball is hurtling through the air! I cringe as he flies over the Tilt-a-Whirl, just misses the Orbiter, and passes straight through the Loop de Loop before SMASHING into Gigantox's massive forehead.

"Ouch," Skunk Girls says, crinkling her nose. "That'll leave a mark."

Gigantox staggers over the bumper cars and falls backward, casting a large shadow over a row of Porta Potty's just as two kids step out. Holy cow! They'll be crushed! There's no time to lose!

I borrow Night Owl's power, grab a shadow off the pavement, and pull the kids to safety with a shadow fist seconds before Gigantox CRASHES down on top of the bathroom stalls.

"Are you guys okay?" I ask, opening the shadow fist.

"See," one kid says to the other. "I told you the carnival would be more exciting this year."

"Now what, boss-man?" Skunk Girl asks. "We got the bad guy."

"Yes, you did," comes a gritty, familiar voice. "But maybe not in the most efficient way possible. GISMO 2.0, end training module."

"Training module ended, Shadow Hawk," comes GISMO 2.0's warm, mechanical voice.

Just then, everything around us, including Gigantox, the carnival, and the two kids I just rescued all disappear, and we're standing in an enormous, stark white Combat Room 2.0.

"Wait, where'd the carnival go?" Pinball asks, lying flat on his back and looking confused.

"It was all part of the simulation, numbskull," Skunk Girl says. "None of it was real."

"So, does that mean I'm not getting my funnel cake cheeseburgers?" Pinball asks with sadness in his voice.

Believe me, I understand why Pinball is disappointed. TechnocRat built the Combat Room 2.0 to be even more realistic than the original Combat Room—and that's saying something! With all of the upgraded sensory technology he added, it's even harder to accept what you're experiencing isn't real, including the smell of deep-fried Oreos.

"It's time for your evaluation," Shadow Hawk says, flipping through papers on his clipboard. "Glory Girl, would you like to go first?"

I respect Shadow Hawk so much I'll be crushed if we let him down—which I'm pretty sure we did. But I take one look at Grace approaching and brace myself. This could get ugly.

"Yeah, I'll go first," she says, throwing her clipboard over her shoulder. "Let me give it to you straight. You guys stunk out there."

"Then I did my job," Skunk Girl says with a smile.

"That wasn't a compliment," Grace says, her face red with anger. "You may have been in a simulation, but stuff like that could happen in the real world. Sure, you took out the villain, but none of you noticed the people on the Ferris wheel. If you're not completely aware of everything around you, then innocent people will get hurt."

Grace's criticism may be sharp but it's accurate. We never should have engaged with Gigantox until we were sure everyone was safe. I feel like a total failure.

"We blew it," Pinball sighs. "Again."

"Look, don't be so hard on yourselves," Shadow Hawk says. "That's why you're practicing in a safe environment. Things don't always go according to plan, but Glory Girl was spot on that you need to be more aware of your surroundings." Then, he looks down at Pinball and adds, "And not get distracted."

"Sorry about that," Pinball mutters sheepishly.

"That being said," Shadow Hawk continues, "once you recognized the danger you reacted well. Epic Zero made a great tactical suggestion for the slingshot maneuver, and Night Owl and Pinball executed it to perfection."

"Gee, thanks," Pinball says, perking up.

"However, no one checked the bathroom stalls for possible civilians," Shadow Hawk says. "So, clearly, there's more work to do. Remember, practice makes progress. The more you work together the more you'll trust each other. Then, before you know it, you'll anticipate what each other will do without even saying a word. And that's when you know you've become a truly harmonious team. Overall, you should be proud of yourselves. That was a very challenging training module."

Even though Shadow Hawk is being encouraging, I still feel like a heel. After all, I'm the team leader, so if I fail I take the team down with me. Plus, I know this mission would be considered a disaster by Freedom Force standards. If we want to be great we'll have to keep practicing.

"Alert! Alert! Alert!" the Meta Monitor blares. "Meta 3 disturbance. Repeat: Meta 3 disturbance. Power signature identified as The Freaks of Nature. Alert! Alert! Alert! Meta 3 disturbance. Meta signature identified as The Freaks of Nature."

"Freedom Force to Mission Room," comes Dad's voice over the intercom system. "Freedom Force to Mission Room."

"Holy smokes!" Pinball says. "Was that a real Meta alert? With real Meta villains? Can we go?"

"I'm afraid not," Shadow Hawk says, pushing a few buttons on his utility belt. "Captain Justice, this is Shadow Hawk. Glory Girl and I have Next Gen in the Combat

Room for training. Give us a few minutes to escort them to the Hangar so they can return to Earth."

"Roger, Shadow Hawk," comes Dad's voice. "But why don't you guys keep training and I'll handle it with the rest of the team. Besides, someone needs to stay behind because it looks like we'll be in deep space and potentially off the grid for a while. Oh, and keep Glory Girl with you. This is good leadership training for her."

"What? Are you kidding me?" Grace exclaims. "Haven't I been tortured enough?"

"Roger, Captain," Shadow Hawk says with a smile. "We're happy to continue here. Well, at least most of us. Good luck."

"Roger," Dad says. "You too." Then, he clicks off.

"Well," Shadow Hawk says, looking at us, "should we try another training module?"

"Absolutely," I say, more determined to get it right than ever. "I want to nail this one. What do you guys say?"

"I'm in," Selfie says.

"Me too," Night Owl says.

"Okey-dokey," Skunk Girl says.

"I suppose," Pinball says, still lying flat on his back. "But can't a guy get a funnel cake cheeseburger around here first?"

TWO

I FILE A MISSING PERSONS REPORT

So, we didn't nail the second run.

In fact, we did even worse. The thing is, I actually thought GISMO 2.0 went easy on us. All we had to do was catch a pair of Meta 2 villains called Fire and Lice who were hiding out in the Keystone City Aquarium. Everything started out okay, but then it all went downhill faster than an elephant on skis.

First, Skunk Girl had to use the bathroom. Then, Night Owl nearly knocked herself unconscious. And finally, not to be outdone, Pinball bounced right past the villains and shattered the shark tank. Seconds later, we were trying not to drown in the deluge of water while the bad guys got away.

So, yeah, not stellar.

After that, everyone went home and I went to bed. Except, I can't sleep. I've been tossing and turning all night, and this time it's not Dog-Gone's fault, even though he's snoring so loud the walls are shaking. I've tried everything to get some shut-eye, from saying the alphabet backward to counting sheep, but no matter what I do I can't stop thinking about our pathetic performance in the Combat Room. That and the look of sheer disappointment on Shadow Hawk's face.

This time, Grace was even more brutal in her critique of our performance and Shadow Hawk didn't say much of anything. Not that he had to, his frown said it all.

According to Shadow Hawk, we'll need to trust each other for our team to work, and if that's the case then maybe we've been doomed from the start. I mean, we haven't had a successful mission yet—so who's responsible for that?

Unfortunately, I know the answer.

Awesome.

Since I'm not sleeping I might as well go for a walk. I carefully peel down the covers so I don't disturb Dog-Gone when I remember I'm still in my costume. I was so bummed out I didn't have the energy to put on my pajamas. Then, I notice the clock which reads 3:13 a.m.

Great. At least the halls should be empty.

As I make my way through the residential wing I

notice my parents' bedroom door is still open, which means they're not back yet. I guess fighting the Freaks of Nature was more challenging than they thought.

I grab a snack from the Galley, loop around the Trophy Room, and saunter past the Medi-wing. That's when I notice that the light in the Monitor Room is on. That's strange. Usually, we let the Meta Monitor do its thing overnight. So, either someone forgot to turn out the light or someone is in there right now.

Since Dog-Gone is unconscious on my bed, there are only two people it could be, and I've never known Grace to skimp on her beauty sleep. I head up the stairs and when I reach the top I find Shadow Hawk sitting in the command chair. What's he doing up so late?

"Hey, kid," he says, not even turning around. "I didn't know you were a sleepwalker."

"I'm not," I say. "I just can't sleep. What about you? Why are you up?"

"I try to get as little sleep as possible," he says, rotating his chair towards me. "Too many nightmares. So, what's keeping you up?"

"Oh, nothing," I say, letting out a deep sigh. "Well, I… I guess I keep thinking about our Combat Room training. We just can't get it together… and it's all my fault."

"How so?" he asks.

"I'm the leader," I say. "So, if we fail it's on me. And I can't seem to get us working as a team."

"I see," Shadow Hawk says, his pointer finger tapping his chiseled chin. "Well, the leader does set the tone for the team. But it's also impossible for a team to function if they don't have a common goal. To be successful as a team everyone has to work together in harmony."

"Yeah," I say. "That makes sense."

"Look, I've been on teams that fell apart because everyone did their own thing," Shadow Hawk says. "But I've also been a part of great teams, like the Freedom Force, where everyone works towards the same goal. And because of that, we trust each other implicitly. Maybe you should see if everyone is on the same page."

Suddenly, a light bulb goes off. Maybe that's where we're going wrong. Maybe we're not all on the same page. I mean, I want us to be the best Meta team ever but do the others want the same thing? Sometimes I think all Pinball wants to do is eat. And Skunk Girl can run hot or cold depending on the minute. Night Owl is still a mystery to me. But Selfie… I know she's with me.

"I… I never thought of it that way," I say. "Thanks."

"No problem, kid," Shadow Hawk says. "I know you'll figure it out. Just don't give up on—"

"Alert! Alert! Alert!" the Meta Monitor blares. "Meta 3 disturbance. Repeat: Meta 3 disturbance. Power signature identified as Warrior Woman. Alert! Alert! Alert! Meta 3 disturbance. Meta signature identified as Warrior Woman."

"Warrior Woman?" Shadow Hawk mutters, his face

turning pale. "But... that's impossible."

For a second, I'm taken aback. I mean, I don't think I've ever seen Shadow Hawk look as white as a ghost before. And as he spins back around in his chair I wrack my brain for where I've heard the name 'Warrior Woman' before. For some reason, it sounds familiar. And then—

"Alert! Alert! Alert!" the Meta Monitor blares. "Meta 3 disturbance. Repeat: Meta 3 disturbance. Identity unknown. Alert! Alert! Alert! Meta 3 disturbance. Identity unknown."

Identity unknown?

"It's coming from the Isle of Alala," Shadow Hawk says, his voice sounding urgent. Then, he pounds his fist on the keyboard and leaps from his chair. "I've got to go."

"The Isle of Alala?" I say. "Isn't that an island in the Pacific Ocean that's home to a group of super-strong Meta women?"

Suddenly, everything clicks.

Holy cow! I know exactly who Warrior Woman is!

"Um, hang on," I say. "Isn't that, like, *the* Warrior Woman? As in, one of the founders of the Protectors of the Planet? As in, the greatest superhero team of the Golden Age of Metas?"

"One and the same," Shadow Hawk says, bounding down the stairs, his black cape billowing behind him. "And she needs my help."

"Not just your help," I say, running down behind

him. "Our help!"

***

As we fly across the Pacific Ocean, I try engaging Shadow Hawk in conversation, but he's lost in thought. Not that I can blame him. I mean, I can't believe I'm actually going to meet Warrior Woman, an original member of the Protectors of the Planet! A few years ago, Shadow Hawk showed me his collection of old newspaper clippings about the team. And Dad is such a Meta history buff he'd flip if he knew where we were going! I kind of feel bad Grace is still sleeping, but hey, you snooze you lose.

But then I realize something.

Warrior Woman has got to be pretty old by now.

I mean, she was a big hero back in the Golden Age, which was, like, forty years ago. The Protectors of the Planet were the premier superhero team of their time before the Freedom Force even existed. The seven original members are legends within the Meta community.

There was Warrior Woman, of course. She came to America as an ambassador for peace but often had to put her formidable fighting skills to use. Then, there was Riptide, Prince of the lost city of Atlantis. He could control water and breathe on both land and sea. And who could forget Will Power, an Earth-born galactic guardian who defended the planet with a magic, alien rock.

An experiment gone wrong gave Goldrush the power of Super-Speed, while the Black Crow was a Meta 0 vigilante who patrolled the night and protected the innocent from evil. His Meta 0 sidekick, Sparrow, was just a boy but his combat skills nearly rivaled his mentor. And last but not least was Meta-Man, the most powerful hero of them all.

Meta-Man came to Earth from an unknown planet. He was called Meta-Man for a reason because he could use different types of Meta powers, but only one at a time. And based on his green costume he earned the nickname 'the Emerald Enforcer.'

As legend has it, all of these heroes came together for the first time to take on a dangerous villain called the Soul Snatcher. After that, they decided to band together to defend the planet from future threats, and that's how the Protectors of the Planet was formed.

Meta-Man was the leader, and over time other heroes joined the team, like Sergeant Stretch, a Meta-morph who could stretch his body into various shapes, and the Marksman, who never missed his target. But according to Dad, Meta-Man left Earth after a mission went horribly wrong and no one has seen him since.

Once Meta-Man took off, the rest of the Protectors went their separate ways. A few of them stayed in the hero game for a little while longer before eventually leaving the scene. I wonder if Shadow Hawk ever met any of the Protectors in person? I'm about to ask him when he says—

"We're here."

I look down to see a lush island sitting in the middle of the ocean. It looks beautiful from up high, and as we get closer I see cobblestone roads and temple-like structures made of white marble. It's impressive, like it was transported here from ancient Greece, but unfortunately, that's not all I see, because there's a giant plume of black smoke coming from the city's center.

"Prepare for landing," Shadow Hawk says gruffly, angling the Freedom Flyer towards the disturbance.

As we head for the smoke, I see marble slabs scattered everywhere. There's no doubt something major happened here. The question is *what?* Shadow Hawk spins us around and touches down in a small clearing near the debris.

But before we exit to investigate, he puts a hand on my arm and says, "Be alert. As far as I'm aware, only Warrior Woman and her husband still live here. No one else has stepped foot on this island in decades. And her husband doesn't have powers."

"Got it," I say, following him out of the Freedom Flyer. I can't help but notice how strange he's acting. I mean, why is he so freaked out?

But as we approach the rubble I realize Shadow Hawk's cause for concern is justified because the broken marble is super thick. Whoever knocked these buildings down must be pretty darn powerful.

"Look at this," Shadow Hawk says, calling me over to a wall that's still standing. Then, he points to a red, smoldering line cut across its face. It's like it was shot with some sort of a laser or something. But as I step around to get a closer look the back of my head SLAMS into something that knocks me to my knees.

"Ouch!" I say, rubbing my noggin which is absolutely throbbing. What was that?

"Are you okay?" Shadow Hawk asks, pulling me up to my feet. Then, I notice the nose of a green, single-flyer airplane behind him. "Warrior Woman's War-Jet," he says.

"Right," I say. I completely forgot that Warrior Woman couldn't fly and used a jet to get around.

"If her War-Jet is still here," Shadow Hawk says, "then it means she didn't get away. So, either she's buried under all of this rubble or—"

"Help!" comes a man's voice.

We spin around to find a very old man hobbling towards us on crutches. His snow-white beard contrasts against his red, sun-burned skin, and his clothes are tattered and torn.

"Mr. Henson?" Shadow Hawk says. "Is that you?"

Mr. Henson? Is that Warrior Woman's husband?

"P-Please," the man says, speaking quickly with sheer panic in his eyes. "Y-You have to save her. H-He took her! He said he... wanted revenge!"

"Mr. Henson, please, slow down," Shadow Hawk

says. "Who took her? Who wanted revenge?"

The old man looks at us but nothing comes out of his mouth. He looks terrified.

"It's okay, Mr. Henson," Shadow Hawk says, putting his hand on the man's shoulder. "Just tell us what you saw."

"H-He looked the same as he did all those years ago," Mr. Henson finally says. "Like he... never aged. Even after all this time. And... he took her."

"Who?" Shadow Hawk asks. "Who didn't age? Who took her?"

"M-Meta-Man," Mr. Henson blurts out. "Meta-Man took my wife. M-Meta-Man is back!"

THREE

I GET A FUNNY FEELING

Meta-Man.

Before he left Earth he was one of the greatest heroes of all time. But now, according to Warrior Woman's husband, he's back—and for some reason, he just ambushed and kidnapped Warrior Woman!

But why?

I mean, Mr. Henson, Warrior Woman's husband said Meta-Man is back for revenge. But for revenge against who? I mean, Warrior Woman was his teammate. What did she ever do to him?

I try picking Shadow Hawk's brain on our trip back to the Waystation 2.0 but he's not very talkative. He's probably as shocked as I am by what happened. After all, he idolizes the Protectors of the Planet.

The only thing he did clear up for me is why the Meta Monitor didn't identify Meta-Man's power signature in the first place. Apparently, Meta-Man left the planet way before TechnocRat built the Meta Monitor, so it never had the chance to register his Meta signature. Meta-Man has a data profile only because Shadow Hawk added it to the database himself.

Even though Mr. Henson gave us an eyewitness account of what happened, Shadow Hawk still wants to make sure it's accurate. That's why we're bringing one of the burned marble slabs back to the Waystation for analysis. Shadow Hawk wants to feed it into the Meta Spectrometer to confirm the type of Meta power that caused the laser marks. And if he can do that, we may be able to track Meta-Man himself.

I sure hope it works, because if what Mr. Henson said is true, Meta-Man clearly didn't come back for a team reunion. There's definitely more to this story, and as soon as we get back to the Waystation I'll see what else I can find out. But as we pull into the Hangar, two familiar figures are waiting for us—one wagging his tail and the other looking like she wants to clobber somebody.

"Um, what's up with Grace?" I ask.

"I don't know," Shadow Hawk says, parking the Freedom Flyer in its usual spot. "But I see the others aren't back yet."

Huh? Then, I notice the empty parking spot next to

us. He's right, the Freedom Flyer my parents took is still gone. Gee, I hope they're okay. But when I look down at Grace's angry face I suspect I'd rather be with them right now, wherever they are.

"I'm going to start the analysis," Shadow Hawk says, popping the hatch and hoisting the marble slab over his shoulder. "Good luck."

"Thanks," I say, swallowing hard. "I think I'm going to need it."

As soon as I step off the ramp, Dog-Gone jumps up and starts licking my face. And then—

"Well, well, nice of you to come back," Grace says with her arms crossed. "Guess who didn't get any sleep last night?"

"You mean, other than Shadow Hawk and me?" I answer. "Because in case you didn't notice, we just got back from a mission that started in the wee hours of the morning."

"Funny you should mention 'wee,'" Grace says. "Because your stupid dog started howling for the bathroom right after you left."

"He did, did he?" I say, kneeling to scratch his neck. "You had to go, didn't you, boy?"

"Yeah, he had to go," Grace says. "And after he woke me up from a dead sleep and I took him, he crawled into my bed and stole all of my covers! So, I'll tell you who didn't get enough sleep. Me!"

"Okay, okay, I'm sorry," I say, heading for the exit.

"But you'll have to excuse me because there's something I've got to look into."

"Elliott Harkness, get back here!" Grace calls out. "I'm not done yelling at you yet!"

"Gosh, that sure sounds like fun," I say, pushing open the Hangar door, "but I've got to run. You see, Meta-Man just kidnapped Warrior Woman so there are a few things I've gotta do."

"Meta-Man kidnapped Warrior Woman?" Grace says. "As in, *the* Meta-Man and Warrior Woman? Hey, hold on!"

I hear Grace's footsteps behind me and when I turn around she's hot on my tail asking for the lowdown on everything that just happened. By the time I fill her in, we've reached the Mission Room. I hop into the command chair and start typing into the keyboard.

"What are you doing?" she asks.

"Finding out more about Meta-Man," I say. "Shadow Hawk told me a little bit about him, but I don't know his whole story."

Suddenly, words start scrolling down the screen:

- *Name: Meta-Man.*
- *History: Very little is known about the origin of Meta-Man. He was born on a distant planet in an unknown galaxy. As a toddler, he was sent to Earth in a spaceship. The reasons for why he was sent to Earth are unknown. His ship landed near Houston where it was discovered by a corrupt oil baron named Maximillian Murdock and his*

wife Sophia. The Murdock family adopted the boy and gave him the name Lucas Murdock. During his youth, the Murdocks discovered that Lucas' skin was impervious to harm, making him invulnerable at all times. As he grew older, Lucas developed many other Meta abilities, including Super-Strength, Super-Speed, Heat Vision, Enhanced Senses, and Flight. However, unlike his invulnerability, he was only able to use one of these newly gained Meta powers at a time. His adopted father tried to get Lucas to use his powers for the benefit of his growing criminal empire, but Lucas rejected his father's wishes and left his home behind. He moved to Keystone City, donned a costume to fight crime, and became the superhero known as Meta-Man.

- *Recent Activity: Meta-Man left Earth and has not been seen for many decades.*

"Wow," Grace says. "I didn't know Meta-Man had a father like that."

"Yeah," I say, "me neither. I mean, imagine being sent as a baby to another planet and then being raised by a criminal. But clearly, Meta-Man was always a hero at heart because he rejected his father's evil ways. Talk about brave. He was a hero through and through."

"Correction," comes a voice from behind us. "He *was* a hero, but not anymore."

We turn to see Shadow Hawk standing in the doorway behind us.

"Then it's true?" I ask. "Meta-Man took Warrior Woman?"

"Yes," Shadow Hawk says. "The Meta Spectrometer confirmed it. Those burn marks on the marble slab came from Heat Vision—just like Meta-Man has. Unfortunately, Warrior Woman was an easy target because everyone knows she makes her home on the Isle of Alala. But the other living members of the Protectors of the Planet will be harder to find."

"Living members?" I repeat. "You mean, some of the Protectors have died?"

"Yes," Shadow Hawk says. "Riptide was killed during a challenge for the throne of Atlantis. And Will Power died of old age. But I believe Goldrush, Sergeant Stretch, the Marksman, and the Black Crow are still alive, and I intend to track them down before Meta-Man finds them."

"So, wait," Grace says. "You think Meta-Man will go after them too?"

"I do," Shadow Hawk says. "If Meta-Man took Warrior Woman, I'm positive the others are next. That is, if he hasn't gotten to them already."

"But how will you find them?" I ask. "Those heroes haven't been active for years."

"I'm going to put my detective skills to work," Shadow Hawk says. "And I won't rest until I find them all."

"We can help," Grace says.

"No," Shadow Hawk says. "It's too dangerous. If Meta-Man is this unstable he could wipe you out in the blink of an eye. It's better if I handle this alone."

"Well, what should we do?" I ask.

"You should stay here where it's safe," he says.

"But I don't get it," Grace says. "Why is Meta-Man even doing this? Why is he looking for revenge against his old teammates?"

But instead of answering, Shadow Hawk simply purses his lips and says, "I'll return later."

And then he's gone.

"Well, that was weird," Grace says.

"Yeah," I say. "He's been acting funny since this whole thing started. I mean, I know he really looked up to Meta-Man and the Protectors. Maybe this is freaking him out or something?"

"Maybe," she says, her eyes narrowing. "Or maybe something else is going on. But the last thing I'm going to do is sit here twiddling my thumbs until we hear from Shadow Hawk. Move over."

"Hey!" I say as Grace nudges me right out of the command chair. "What are you doing?"

"Looking for dirt on the Protectors of the Planet," she says, typing into the keyboard. "Shadow Hawk isn't the only one who's good at detective work. Especially when I combine my big brain with the brain of this super-computer. Let's see who can find them first."

"Well, I hate to break it to you," I say, "but just because you have a big head doesn't mean you have a big brain."

"Go away, neanderthal-boy," she says. "And take

your saber-toothed dog with you. This room is for smart people only."

"Very funny," I say. "C'mon, Dog-Gone, let's give her some space. She'll need it to fill all the emptiness in her big head."

"You'll eat those words when I find them first!" she calls out.

"I won't be holding my breath!" I call back, as Dog-Gone and I head down the hallway.

Honestly, I'm happy to go because I could use a nap. The lack of sleep is really starting to catch up with me. But something is bugging me about our conversation with Shadow Hawk. Unfortunately, my head is so fuzzy I can't put my finger on it.

We make our way back to the residential wing and I enter my room. I just need twenty minutes of sleep and I'll feel like a new superhero. I lay down on my bed and Dog-Gone plops down by my feet.

"Make sure you stay down there," I say, closing my eyes. "This time I need the rest."

Okay, just twenty minutes. That's all I—

BEEP!

My eyes pop open. What's that?

BEEP!

I look at my alarm clock but that's not it.

BEEP!

Just then, I realize it's coming from my Next Gen transmitter watch, which means the team needs me! I pull my wrist close to look at the message, which reads:

<Selfie: Epic Zero, team meeting at Hangout.>

Team meeting?

What do we need a team meeting for? I sit up and rub my eyes. Then, I type:

<Right now?>

<Selfie: Yes. Right now.>

Well, that was clear. Suddenly, I have a bad feeling about this. I type back:

<Ok. Leaving in a few min.>

Well, so much for a nap. I put my feet on the floor and stand up. "C'mon, boy," I say to Dog-Gone. "You can make sure I don't fall asleep while I'm flying."

Dog-Gone and I head back the way we came and poke our heads into the Mission Room. Grace is still at the controls toggling between a bunch of data screens.

"I'm heading to Earth for a meeting at the Hangout," I say.

"Uh-huh," Grace says, not even turning around.

"I'm not sure when I'll be back," I say.

"Uh-huh," she says again.

"There's a giant squid on your head," I say.

"Uh-huh," she repeats.

Right. Well, hopefully, she heard what I said because I'd hate for Mom and Dad to get back and not know where I am. But I figure I shouldn't be gone too long anyway. At least, I hope not.

We head back to the Hangar and hop into a Freedom

Ferry. Dog-Gone shuffles into the passenger seat and I buckle us both in. I enter the coordinates for the Hangout, power up the Freedom Ferry, and we're off.

As soon as we hit outer space, it dawns on me that this little meeting might be about me. I mean, what if the team wants to dump me as their leader? Or maybe they want to dump me altogether!

Ugh. Suddenly, I feel sick to my stomach.

But then again, it could be about anything.

I mean, maybe they're tired of being mentored by the Freedom Force. After all, we promised we wouldn't fight in public without the Freedom Force's supervision. Maybe they don't want to do that anymore. Not that I blame them. I mean, we're kids but we're heroes too.

Wait a second.

Kid. Heroes?

Suddenly, I realize what's been bugging me about our conversation with Shadow Hawk. Strangely, he talked about finding all of the living members of the Protectors of the Planet except for one.

For some reason, he didn't say anything about Sparrow.

FOUR

I BRACE MYSELF FOR BAD NEWS

Why didn't Shadow Hawk mention Sparrow?

I know Sparrow was just the Black Crow's sidekick when the Protectors of the Planet were doing their thing, but he was still an original member of the team. With everything going on, did Shadow Hawk forget about him because he was just a kid? The fact that Shadow Hawk didn't even mention him kind of ruffles my feathers.

After all, I'm a kid hero too.

I think I'd be pretty disappointed if people forgot about me. I mean, I've done a few things to save the universe. You know, like getting rid of two Orbs of Oblivion, stopping Ravager from eating the planet, and kicking the Skelton Emperor off of Earth.

You'd think you'd be remembered for stuff like that.

Anyway, before I land at the Hangout, I should probably call Grace to clue her in about Sparrow. I'm sure she's still in the Mission Room because she seemed pretty determined to find the other living Protectors before Shadow Hawk. Maybe she can find Sparrow.

"Freedom Ferry to Waystation," I call into the communicator.

"Roger, Freedom Ferry," comes Grace's exasperated voice. "Why are you bugging me now?"

"I'm not bugging you," I say, rolling my eyes. "I'm letting you know that Shadow Hawk forgot to mention one of the original Protectors."

"Yeah, I know," Grace says. "I'm already looking for Sparrow."

"You are?" I say surprised.

"Of course, I am," she says. "Big brain here, remember?"

Somehow, I manage not to grunt out loud.

"I've already tapped into several databases looking for info on Sparrow," she continues. "Old newspaper articles, police reports, hospital records. He was much younger than the other Protectors so I'm hoping to turn up something. So far I haven't had much luck."

"Okay," I say. "Well, I wasn't sure if you knew so I just thought I'd check."

"Right," she says firmly. "Again, amazing brain here."

"Got it," I say. "And in case you forgot I'm heading

to Earth for a meeting at—"

"Over and out," she says, ending the transmission.

"—the Hangout," I finish meekly. "Over and out," I say, apparently to no one in particular.

Well, she clearly doesn't want to be bothered. And speaking of being bothered, I still don't know what this meeting at the Hangout is about, but something tells me it's not going to be good. In fact, I have a sinking feeling this might be my last appearance as the leader of Next Gen. I find a clearing in the woods behind Selfie's house and land the Freedom Ferry.

"Alright, Dog-Gone," I say, unbuckling my furry companion. "Let's go face the music."

We walk into Selfie's backyard and I look at our treehouse headquarters for quite possibly the very last time. I don't know what I'll do if they want to get rid of me. I mean, these guys are the only friends I've got.

I grab a rung on the ladder when I realize I've got another problem on my hands. Dog-Gone hates climbing ladders. "Oh, come on you big baby," I say. "Get over here."

Dog-Gone backs up quickly, but before he can take off, a shadow wraps around his body like a harness and lifts him off the ground!

"Night Owl?" I say, looking up.

"Don't worry, I've, ugh, got him," she says, struggling to pull him up to the treehouse landing. "But you might want to put him, ugh, on a diet."

"Please, don't say the 'D-word,'" Pinball says as I reach the top of the ladder. "Some of us are simply blessed with more of ourselves than others."

It's great to hear everyone being so cheerful, but as soon as I step onto the landing their faces get serious. Okay, that's not a good sign. I put on a fake smile and say, "So, what's this urgent meeting about anyway?"

"We... need to talk," Selfie says. "As a group. Maybe you should sit down."

"Well, that sounds ominous," I say, taking a seat between Skunk Girl and Night Owl. "So, what do we need to talk about?"

But instead of just coming out with it, Selfie looks down and there's awkward silence. Well, if she can't tell me it can only mean one thing. They're going to fire me as leader.

"Look, boss-man, we need to be honest with you," Skunk Girl says, finally breaking the ice.

Uh-oh, here it comes. I brace myself.

"You're a great hero," she continues. "I mean, you're a member of the Freedom Force for Pete's sake, and... well, we're just a bunch of inexperienced rookies. The truth is, we've realized we probably won't ever reach your level. So, we don't want to hold you back anymore. We think you should dump us."

"What?" I blurt out, totally confused.

They want me to dump them?

But that's crazy!

"Yeah," Selfie says. "We all reached the same conclusion after that second training session. None of us are as fast on our feet as you are, and we certainly can't control our powers like you do. So, why should we make you wait around until we're ready? You could be doing so much more fighting alongside the Freedom Force instead of slumming around with us. We appreciate all the time you've put into trying to make us better, but it's not right for us to drag you down."

"Yeah, you're like, a major Meta," Pinball adds. "You gotta do you, even if that means doing it without us."

I open my mouth to respond but I'm so shocked I can't even find the words. I mean, I appreciate how highly they think of me, but dumping them is the last thing I want to do.

"Sorry we're springing this on you like this," Selfie says, "but we didn't think it was fair to waste any more of your valuable time. Of course, we understand if you don't want to talk to us again."

She looks up at me and I see tears welling in her blue eyes. In fact, the whole team looks sad—even Skunk Girl. I need to put a stop to this.

"Look, guys," I say, "I'm not sure where you're getting this from, but I don't want to leave our team."

"Y-You don't?" Selfie asks.

"No," I say. "I don't. Not even a little bit."

"For real?" Pinball asks. "You're not just saying that because you're a big-time hero and don't want to hurt our feelings?"

"No," I say. "First, I'm no big-time hero. I mean, yeah, I've had some successful missions, but I've messed up plenty too. Second, we're going to get better at this—all of us—but we can't give up. The Freedom Force wasn't perfect on day one and neither are we. We just have to trust each other, and if we do that, I know we'll get there."

Suddenly, their faces perk up.

"Level with us, Epic Zero," Night Owl says. "You've seen true greatness in action. Do you really think we can get there?"

"I do," I say without hesitation. "I really, really do."

Just then, Dog-Gone yawns loudly.

"Well, maybe not all of us," I say, nodding towards Dog-Gone as everyone laughs.

"So, you still want to hang out with us?" Selfie asks.

"Absolutely," I say. "We're a team until the end. The funny thing is, I thought you guys called this meeting to get rid of me."

"What?" Pinball says. "Are you crazy?"

"Maybe," I say. "I just, well, assumed you wanted a different leader. I'm glad I was wrong."

"Totally wrong," Selfie says. "We'd be lost without you. Why would you even think that way?"

"I don't know," I say. "I guess we all feel insecure sometimes. Even a supposed 'big-time hero' like me."

"Well, I'm glad you're sticking around," Selfie says,

wiping her eyes and flashing a big smile.

"Me too," I say, smiling back, my face feeling flush.

Man, I feel such a crazy mix of happiness and relief I don't know whether to jump with joy or kick myself for wasting all that time getting worked up over this meeting.

Sometimes I'm my own worst enemy.

"Okay, boss-man," Skunk Girl says. "Now that we've got that ironed out, your next order of business is to nail down a not-so-lame battle cry for our team. If you yell out, 'Give us liberty or give us death' one more time I'll have to slug you."

"That wasn't even the worst one," Pinball says. "Do you remember when he yelled 'Cowabunga?' I nearly died of embarrassment."

"Okay, okay," I say. "I get it. Don't worry, it'll come to me. Just give me a few more chances."

MEEP! MEEP! MEEP!

"What's that?" Night Owl asks.

"The police monitor!" Selfie says, running over to turn up the volume.

There's some static, and then—SQUAWK!

"—need immediate assistance!" comes a man's panicked voice. "I-I repeat we are under assault! A Meta villain has penetrated our defenses and is tearing this place apart! Our weapons can't seem to stop him and prisoners are escaping! It won't be long until there's an all-out jailbreak! We need immediate assistance, over!"

Prisoners? Jailbreak?

"Roger, Lieutenant," comes a female dispatcher's voice. "We are sending emergency support ASAP. Squadrons four and seven are on their way to your location. Can you confirm the identity of the assailant so I can contact the Freedom Force, over?"

"Never seen him before!" the Lieutenant says. "Hurry!"

"Stay focused, Lieutenant," the dispatcher says. "Can you describe him for me?"

"Y-Yeah, kind of!" the Lieutenant says. "He's super-fast so it's hard to get a good bead on him! But he's wearing a green costume and flying all over the place busting down walls! He keeps demanding we produce someone named 'Max Mayhem,' but we don't have anyone by that name here! Uh-oh! He sees me! Get here as fast as—!"

CLICK! And then there's nothing but static.

"Lieutenant?" comes the dispatcher's voice. "Lieutenant, can you hear me? If you're still there, I'm reaching out to the Freedom Force now. Do whatever you can to fend off the villain. We can't have a jailbreak at Lockdown Penitentiary."

L-Lockdown Penitentiary?

I swallow hard.

"What do we do now?" Pinball asks. "That mission sounds really serious and we promised the Freedom Force we wouldn't go out in public without them."

The Freedom Force?

OMG! Suddenly, I realize that if my parents and the rest of the team aren't back yet, it'll be up to Shadow Hawk, Grace, and, well, me. And who even knows where Shadow Hawk is right now.

"What's the call, boss-man?" Skunk Girl asks. "Do we kick it to the big guns or handle it ourselves?"

I look at the team and see the hunger in their eyes. But Pinball is right, we told the Freedom Force we wouldn't do anything without them. But then again, this is Lockdown we're talking about. It houses hundreds of super dangerous Meta creeps. And if there's a jailbreak there's no way I could get them all back in their cells on my own.

I-I don't know what to do.

"Boss-man?" Skunk Girl says. "You with us?"

"Um, yeah," I say, snapping back to reality.

"What's the call?" she asks.

I know what we promised my parents, but I don't think I have a choice. I take a deep breath and say—

"Let's go mash some Metas."

"Yahoo!" Skunk Girl yells. "Now there's a battle cry!"

Meta Profile

Warrior Woman

Name: Alexandra Noble	Height: 5'11"
Race: Athenian	Weight: 160 lbs
Status: Hero/Inactive	Eyes/Hair: Brown/Black

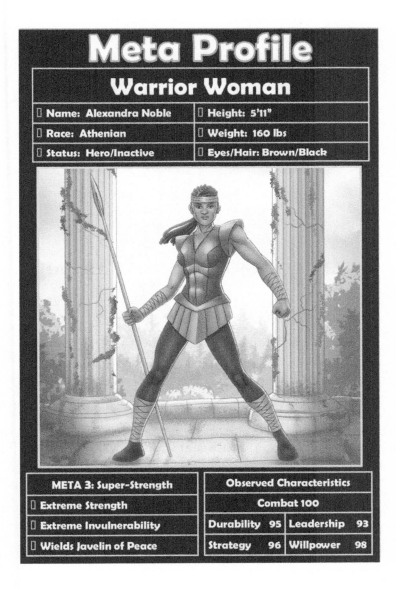

META 3: Super-Strength	Observed Characteristics		
Extreme Strength	Combat 100		
Extreme Invulnerability	Durability 95	Leadership	93
Wields Javelin of Peace	Strategy 96	Willpower	98

FIVE

I CAN'T SEEM TO STAY OUT OF JAIL

I have a feeling I'm going to regret this.

I mean, according to what we heard over the police monitor, some Meta is ripping Lockdown apart with his bare hands. And while we didn't learn the identity of the perpetrator, we did learn he's looking for someone named Max Mayhem, whoever that is. But if this villain is powerful enough to withstand Lockdown's substantial defenses, then he's one seriously strong Meta.

But that's not the only problem we'll face. The police lieutenant said Lockdown was close to a jailbreak. If that happens, hundreds of dangerous Metas could be set free. And to add to the drama, I tried contacting my parents from the Freedom Ferry but there was no answer.

So, that pretty much means we're on our own.

Just. Freaking. Wonderful.

Dog-Gone curls up next to me inside the Freedom Ferry as I check on the rest of the team trailing behind us. I offered to give them a lift but they thought it would look more heroic to storm Lockdown under their own powers. I adjust the rearview camera to find Pinball bouncing alongside Night Owl, who is riding a shadow slide with Selfie and Skunk Girl.

Gotta love their enthusiasm.

I just hope I didn't make a big mistake.

I take a deep breath and breathe out. What was I thinking? I got the team pumped up to tackle this mission, but the more I think about it the more I realize we're biting off more than we can chew.

I was so caught up in the excitement of us staying together that I didn't think this through. I truly believe in our potential as a superhero team, but we're just not there yet. I mean, my own experiences with Lockdown have been nothing but nightmares. From losing K'ami to my strange meeting with Tormentus, nothing ever goes right when I step foot in that place.

So, why would this be any different?

What if we get there to find a massive jailbreak? Can Skunk Girl stop a Meta 3 villain like Side-Splitter? Can Pinball take down Deathblow? Deep down I know the answer, which means I also know what I have to do. But before I do that it would be great to set up some legitimate backup other than Dog-Gone.

So, I swallow my pride and flick on the communicator. "Freedom Ferry to Waystation," I say. "Freedom Ferry to Waystation, do you read me?"

"Roger, Freedom Ferry," Grace says. "Didn't I just tell you not to bug me? I'm kind of busy right now."

"Well, so am I," I say, "because it case you didn't know, there's a Meta destroying—"

"—Lockdown?" Grace says, cutting me off yet again. "Yeah, I know. The Meta Monitor is lit up like a Christmas tree over here and I just hung up with the Keystone City Police. The thing is, the Meta Monitor can't identify the bad guy. The Meta signature is coming back as 'identity unknown.' I've been pinging Shadow Hawk but he's not responding. I've already tried him, like, ten times."

Shadow Hawk isn't responding? That's not like him.

"Well, don't worry," I say, "I'm on the case but, um, could use a little help."

"You're on the what?" Grace says confused. "What do you mean you're on the—? Whoa! Hold on there, bucko! You're not heading to Lockdown are you?"

"Well, yeah," I say. "That's exactly where I'm heading."

"Back off," Grace says. "This one is serious. If you die on my watch Mom will take away my phone forever! Stay put, I'm heading for a Freedom Ferry now!"

"Look, I didn't call you for a babysitter," I say. "I called you for backup. And I can't just sit around until you get here. Every second counts."

"Don't you move!" Grace barks into the communicator. "Do you hear me? I'm getting inside the Freedom Ferry right now."

"What? PSSSSSSHHHHHH!" I say, holding the communicator close to my mouth. "Is that static? I couldn't PSSSSSSHHHHHH you!"

"Don't play games with me!" Grace yells.

"Sorry, I PSSSSSSHHHHHH hear you," I say.

And then I flick off the communicator.

Well, that felt good. But despite my bravado, we both know she's right—this mission has all the makings of a major disaster. But what I didn't tell her is that she's got a few minutes to get down here because there's something I have to do first. I've got to send Next Gen home.

I slow the thrusters on my Freedom Ferry when—

"Alert! Alert! Alert!" the Meta Monitor blares. "Meta 3 disturbance. Repeat: Meta 3 disturbance. Power signature identified as Speed Demon. Alert! Alert! Alert! Meta 3 disturbance. Meta signature identified as Speed Demon."

Speed Demon? But how can that be? I mean, Master Mime put Speed Demon in Lockdown years ago.

And that's when it clicks.

Speed Demon just busted out!

Suddenly, I see a small dust cloud in the distance. Except, it's getting bigger and bigger and heading our way at incredible speed! And then I realize that's no ordinary dust cloud, that's Speed Demon!

I switch on the Freedom Ferry's megaphone and yell out to the team, "Look out!" But in the blink of an eye Speed Demon ZOOMS beneath us, kicking up an intense air current that blows the Freedom Ferry sideways!

Dog-Gone YELPS as we're jerked in our seatbelts, but I manage to turn the steering column and hit the thrusters to level us back off. Thank goodness we're okay, but when I look in the rearview camera the rest of the team is gone! I quickly check my radar to find Pinball miles away but there's no sign of the girls.

Where did they go?

Just then, a gigantic shadow parachute floats down, and Night Owl, Selfie, and Skunk Girl land on my hood.

"What was that?" Night Owl asks, forming a giant shadow slide for her, Selfie, and Skunk Girl.

"Speed Demon!" I yell back. "But look out because there might be—"

"Alert! Alert! Alert!" the Meta Monitor blares. "Meta 2 disturbance. Repeat: Meta 2 disturbance. Power signature identified as Talon. Alert! Alert! Alert! Meta 2 disturbance. Meta signature identified as Talon."

Talon? She's a half-human, half-bird creature who loves to terrorize people. She was also at Lockdown. In fact, Blue Bolt just put her there. Then, I see a black dot in the sky. It's coming towards us. Getting larger.

"Get down!" I yell.

Night Owl, Selfie, and Skunk Girl duck right before a

giant, winged woman BUZZES over their heads and BRUSHES past the Freedom Ferry.

An instant later, she's gone.

"Um, thanks," Selfie says, looking off into the distance with dread. "I'm guessing she came from Lockdown."

"Yep," I say, watching Talon's signal disappear off my radar. Well, here we go. Two major villains just got away scot-free and there was nothing I could do. But if I don't act quickly they'll be just the tip of the iceberg. After all, every second I waste is another second a villain might get free. I've got to get to Lockdown fast, but I can't risk my team getting hurt.

So, here comes the first hard part.

"Team, we need to talk," I say.

"Cool," Skunk Girl says, "let's talk strategy."

I see the excitement in her eyes and I feel crummy, but I've got to do what I've got to do.

"Listen," I say, "we're not talking strategy. I know you're not going to like this, but I've got to pull rank and send you guys home."

"What?" Skunk Girl says, her eyes narrowing.

"Look," I say, "Lockdown is filled with deadly villains like Speed Demon and Talon. Plus, there's a Meta 3 we know nothing about breaking them loose. I know it stinks, but this mission is simply too risky for you guys to be here right now. It's my fault. I'm... really sorry."

"Are you kidding me?" Skunk Girl says. "We're not

sitting this one out. You said we're a team."

"I know what I said," I say, "but you've also trusted me to be your leader. So, as your leader, I'm ordering you to go home before someone gets killed."

"Seriously?" Skunk Girl fires back. "Whatever happened to 'let's go mash some Metas?'"

"Skunk Girl, chill," Selfie says, putting her hand on Skunk Girl's shoulder. "That's clear, Epic. You go ahead. We'll find Pinball and head home, just like you asked."

"Phooey," Skunk Girl says, crossing her arms.

"Thank you," I say to Selfie, "and I'm really sorry."

I see the disappointment written all over Night Owl's face but I can't worry about that now. So, I hit the thrusters and Dog-Gone's ears snap back as we take off. I feel lousy but I didn't have a choice. This has already gotten way too dangerous.

Probably even for me.

"Alert! Alert! Alert!" the Meta Monitor suddenly blares. "Meta 3 disturbance. Repeat: Meta 3 disturbance. Power signature identified as Doc Hurricane. Alert! Alert! Alert! Meta 3 disturbance. Meta signature identified as Doc Hurricane."

Followed by, "Alert! Alert! Alert!" the Meta Monitor blares. "Meta 3 disturbance. Repeat: Meta 3 disturbance. Power signature identified as Lady MacDeath. Alert! Alert! Alert! Meta 3 disturbance. Meta signature identified as Lady MacDeath."

Which is then followed by, "Alert! Alert! Alert!" the

Meta Monitor blares. "Meta 2 disturbance. Repeat: Meta 2 disturbance. Power signature identified as Miss Behave. Alert! Alert! Alert! Meta 2 disturbance. Meta signature identified as Miss Behave."

OMG! Villains are getting loose by the truckload!

"Alert! Alert! Alert!" the Meta Monitor blares yet again. I switch it off quickly so I can concentrate. Criminals are pouring out but there's nothing I can do except try to stop it at the source. I put more power into the thrusters and rocket towards Lockdown on overdrive, but as soon as the facility comes into view I wish I was somewhere else.

Thick, black smoke blankets Lockdown, making it difficult to see what's happening on the ground. Unfortunately, what I can see makes me sick to my stomach, because perimeter walls are leveled, guard towers are destroyed, and three of the eight prison wings are missing roofs! And that's not all, dozens of inmates are streaming out of Lockdown on foot, by air, or in stolen vehicles! And as much as I want to catch them I can't because if I don't stop the villain responsible he'll free hundreds more!

But where is he?

"Hang on, Dog-Gone," I say, "we're going down."

I drop the Freedom Ferry through the black smog and touch down hard on a pile of rubble. I look around but the smoke is so heavy you can't see more than a few feet in front of your face. Yet, I do see a melted police cannon, a smashed armored truck, and a flipped-over police car. But that's not all, because inside that flipped police car is a police officer, and he's still buckled in his seat!

"Be careful," I warn Dog-Gone as I remove his seat belt. Then, I pop the hatch and race to the police car.

"Officer, are you okay?" I ask, reaching through the busted window to gently shake his shoulder. His face is beet red and there's a scar across his forehead where he must have hit the steering wheel. "Officer?" I repeat. "Are you okay?"

Suddenly, his eyelids flutter open.

"W-Where am I?" the officer asks, looking around confused. "Who... Who are you?"

"I'm Epic Zero," I say. "I'm a member of the Freedom Force. Let me help you out of here." I reach for the car door when he says—

"N-No." Then, he nods at something over my shoulder. "D-Don't... help me. H-Help... the girl."

The girl? What girl?

Then, I spin around and gasp, because on the other side of my vehicle is another Freedom Ferry! I didn't see it through the smoke but I nearly landed on top of it! But... it's badly damaged. For some reason, it's smashed into the side of the building!

For a split second, I'm confused where it came from.

And then it hits me like a ton of bricks.

"Is she with you?" comes a deep voice from

overhead.

I look up to find a dark-haired man wearing a green costume with an 'M-M' insignia on his chest. As he stares me down with his piercing blue eyes, I notice a thin scar running across his left cheekbone.

At first, I don't recognize him.

And then I realize who I'm staring at.

It's... Meta-Man!

And then I register what he just asked me.

Because in his arms is the body of an unconscious girl with a crimson costume and white cape.

It's... Grace!

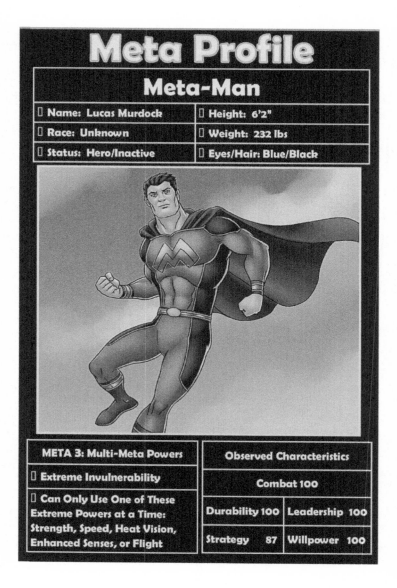

Meta Profile

Meta-Man

▯ Name: Lucas Murdock	▯ Height: 6'2"
▯ Race: Unknown	▯ Weight: 232 lbs
▯ Status: Hero/Inactive	▯ Eyes/Hair: Blue/Black

META 3: Multi-Meta Powers	Observed Characteristics	
▯ Extreme Invulnerability	Combat 100	
▯ Can Only Use One of These Extreme Powers at a Time: Strength, Speed, Heat Vision, Enhanced Senses, or Flight	Durability 100	Leadership 100
	Strategy 87	Willpower 100

SIX

I COME FACE-TO-FACE WITH A LEGEND

I can't keep my jaw from hanging open.

I'm staring at Meta-Man—the greatest Meta hero of all time! But what's he doing here?

I mean, Meta-Man was known as the Emerald Enforcer, and the police lieutenant said the guy who was destroying Lockdown was wearing a green costume. So, this must be Meta-Man alright. But I have to say, I never expected to meet him like this. Especially since he's holding my unconscious sister in his arms.

However, there's something strange about him. It takes me a second to figure it out, but then I realize he still looks like he's in his prime, just like Mr. Henson said. I mean, for a guy who disappeared forty years ago, you'd think he would have aged—a lot! But instead, other than that scar on his face, he's got perfectly smooth skin, thick, black hair, and rippling muscles. He looks exactly like the picture in his Meta profile. It's like he never aged at all.

How is that possible?

But before I can ask him I hear Shadow Hawk's voice inside my head—*if Meta-Man is this unstable he could wipe you out in the blink of an eye.* Suddenly I'm more concerned about what's going on inside Meta-Man's head than how he looks on the outside. With all of his raw power, instability is the last thing I need.

Unfortunately, the evidence before me is as clear as day. Not only did he kidnap Warrior Woman, but now he's crushed Lockdown and he's holding Grace. So, there's only one logical conclusion.

Meta-Man is totally bonkers.

Now that that's out of the way, how do I stop him without risking Grace's life? I mean, his power levels are off the charts. I could try negating his power but he's still super-strong and Grace could get hurt. I need to proceed with extreme caution.

But how?

Then, it dawns on me. He was a hero once. Maybe I can reason with him. "Um, you're Meta-Man," I say profoundly, my voice cracking.

But instead of answering, he just stares at me with a puzzled expression on his face.

"Meta... Man?" he says finally, his eyebrows

furrowing like the wheels inside his head are spinning. Like he's thinking back to a time long, long ago.

"Um, yeah," I say. "That's your name."

"Y-Yes," he says, his face relaxing. "I-I haven't been called that in… many, many years."

Okay, what's up with him? It's like he forgot who he was or something.

"Well, that was you," I say. "I mean, that *is* you. And maybe you also forgot that you're a hero. You were the leader of the Protectors of the Planet—the greatest superhero team of its time."

"The… Protectors of the Planet," he repeats slowly.

"Exactly," I say, "they were your friends, remember?"

"Friends?" he says, but suddenly, he frowns and there's rage in his eyes. "Friends do not betray friends! And now they will pay the ultimate price for their betrayal!"

Okay, I just hit a nerve. For some reason, mentioning the Protectors of the Planet made him very, very angry, which is the last thing I wanted to do. So, I'm thinking I should avoid asking him about Warrior Woman for now. And why does he think the Protectors betrayed him? I'm dying to know, but my first priority is to rescue Grace. I need to get this conversation back on track.

"Hey, you're clearly upset," I say, extending my open palms toward him. "No one wants to be betrayed. But guess what, we're not them. In fact, I'm a hero, just like you. And so is the girl you're holding. My name is Epic Zero and she's Glory Girl—although between us she's really not that glorious—but we're both members of the Freedom Force, the greatest superhero team of this era. So, how about you put her down gently and we can talk some things through?"

"She fired weapons at me," Meta-Man says. "She tried to harm me."

Darn it, Grace. As usual, you're not exactly making it easy for me to save your life.

"Well, maybe you should look at this from our perspective," I say, trying to sound upbeat. "You didn't exactly tell anyone you were coming back to Earth, did you? And while we're absolutely thrilled to meet a legend like you, even you have to admit it kind of looks like you're trying to free all the prisoners here. So, you can see our conundrum, right?"

"I want Max Mayhem," Meta-Man says. "Bring him to me and I will give you the girl."

"Right," I say. "That sounds fair. I just have one little question. Who the heck is Max Mayhem?"

"Don't play games with me," Meta-Man says.

"I wish I was playing a game," I say. "But the truth is, you've been gone for a really long time and there isn't anybody named Max Mayhem around anymore."

Suddenly, Meta-Man's face turns red.

"I mean, unless he's going by another name now," I

say quickly. "Um, I guess he could have changed his name to Bobby Bedlam or Timmy Turmoil or something catchy like that. Your average villain does it all the time. Sometimes when their big evil plans fall apart, they just trademark a new name, and boom, they're back in business again."

"Max Mayhem is no average villain," Meta-Man says. "He considers himself to be the most intelligent human on Earth. His only goal is world domination and he will stop at nothing until he achieves it. I must find him. He... took something from me."

Wow, did I just hear his voice waver? Whatever this Max Mayhem character took must have meant a lot to Meta-Man. The problem is, there's no Max Mayhem here. In fact, I don't ever remember seeing a profile for Max Mayhem. This guy could be long dead for all I know.

But I don't want to tell Meta-Man that.

"Listen, I'm sorry about what he did to you," I say, "but Glory Girl didn't intend to harm you. As I said earlier, we just didn't know who you were or what you were doing here. So, why don't you let her go, and maybe we can look for this Max Mayhem guy together?"

"Together?" Meta-Man says.

"Yes," I say. "You and me. We'll team up just like heroes should. We'll find him together."

"I... I must find him," Meta-Man says, his eyebrows softening and his lips quivering.

Holy smokes, I think I'm getting through to him.

"So, let's just put her down carefully," I continue, "and we can get started."

Meta-Man hesitates and then lowers himself.

Yes! It's working! It's—

"COW-A-BUNG-A!"

Um, Cowa-what?

Suddenly, a round object comes bouncing out of the smog, heading straight for Meta-Man!

Oh. No.

BOOM!

Before I can react, Pinball SLAMS into Meta-Man, sending Grace flying out of his arms! As Meta-Man hurtles headfirst into a wall, I make like a world-class wide receiver and track Grace's body until it lands limply in my arms, sending us both crashing to the ground.

Needless to say, I take the full brunt of the fall.

"Glory Girl, wake up!" I yell, shaking her shoulder as she lays sprawled on top of me. "It's Meta-Man! We've got to get out of here!"

But Grace only moans.

Well, at least she's not dead. I push her arm off my forehead and roll her onto her back. She's gonna owe me big time after this one. But then again, I wasn't the one who saved her. Although she might regret not being dead when she finds out who did.

"No one messes with my girl!" Pinball yells to Meta-Man, who is buried beneath a pile of rubble.

Yep, she's definitely gonna wish she were dead.

But what's Pinball even doing here? I thought the rest of the team went to find him before going home.

"There you are, Pinball!" Selfie says, suddenly appearing out of the smoke with Night Owl and Skunk Girl in tow. "We've been looking all over for—" Then, she sees me lying next to Grace, waves awkwardly, and says, "Oh, hey there, Epic. How's it going?"

Are. You. Kidding. Me?

Now the whole team is here! And Pinball just ruined all of my work calming Meta-Man down. If these guys don't get out of here fast, it's going to be a blood—

"You will pay for that," comes Meta-Man's voice.

—bath.

I look over my shoulder to find Meta-Man on his feet dusting himself off. We're out of time!

"Run!" I yell to the team. "Get out of—!"

But before I can say another word, there's a green blur and POW! Suddenly, Pinball is rocketing sky-high!

"Well, I'm not looking for him again," Skunk Girl says, watching Pinball's body disappear in the distance.

"Focus on the problem at hand, Skunk Girl," Night Owl says, forming a shadow fist and punching Meta-Man.

But Meta-Man holds his ground, and her shadow fist shatters on contact! That's right! Meta-Man is invulnerable as well! And this time he wasn't taken by surprise like when Pinball attacked him.

"My turn," Selfie says, holding up her magic phone. "Now look over here and smile, creep."

But when Meta-Man turns, his eyes are smoldering with a strange red energy!

"Selfie!" I yell. "Look out for his Heat—!"

But I'm too late, as Meta-Man fires his Heat Vision right at Selfie's phone, knocking it out of her hand!

"AAH!" Selfie yells, pulling her hand away as her smoking phone clatters to the ground.

That's it! We won't last another five seconds if this fight continues. So, I concentrate hard and bathe Meta-Man with my negation powers.

Meta-Man turns my way, his eyes blazing with crackling red energy, but then they suddenly go out. Yes, he's powerless! Now we've still got to reel him in. I take a step towards him when I realize something is very wrong.

Why is he smiling at me?

"Neat trick," he says, his eyes narrowing. "Your power probably lets you turn off the powers of ordinary Metas. But my powers don't work like that. You see, I can reallocate my Meta energy instantaneously. So, as soon as I felt something sapping away my Heat Vision, I just shifted my energy from my eyes to my legs. Which means you've lost this race."

Um, what?

Just then, I realize he's about to mow me down with his Super-Speed! I try to move but it's too late as a green blur heads straight for me! But then, a black line shoots across the ground and Meta-Man goes flying into a wall!

What happened? That's when I notice the shadow

tripwire running along the ground.

"Thanks for the save," I say to Night Owl.

"No worries," she says with a wink. "I'll add it to your bill."

"I'm gonna clock that snake when he gets up," Skunk Girl says, pounding a fist into her other hand.

Okay, we've got to get out of here before someone gets seriously hurt—or worse. But how? It's not like we can outrun Meta-Man. Then, I hear a noise, and when I spin around there's a familiar face poking out of the giant hole in the wall Meta-Man just created.

It's X-Port! He's a Meta 3 Energy Manipulator who can teleport from one place to another! Apparently, Meta-Man just busted into the Energy Manipulator wing. Great, just what we needed, more villains on the loose.

"Thanks," X-Port says, stepping over Meta-Man's body and outside his cell to freedom.

Unfortunately, we don't have time to stop X-Port from getting away. I mean, we've got to get out of here ourselves. Plus, there's no way we'd catch him anyway. After all, he can... he can...

OMG! He can teleport!

I concentrate and duplicate as much of X-Port's power as possible. And just as I feel his Meta energy flood my body, X-Port extends his arms and legs into an 'X' shape and a red void appears. Then, he steps inside and disappears!

Well, there goes my power source. I hope I have

enough juice stored up.

"It's time to end this," Meta-Man says, stepping out of the hole in X-Port's prison wall.

Holy Cow! He's back!

"No," I say, "it's time to exit!"

I spread my limbs into an 'X' shape, activate X-Port's teleportation power, and a small, red void appears. I focus hard and push it out with everything I've got, stretching it to envelop Grace, Selfie, Skunk Girl, Night Owl, and Dog-Gone.

"What are you doing?" Meta-Man asks.

"Leaving," I say.

And then I snap the void closed and we're gone.

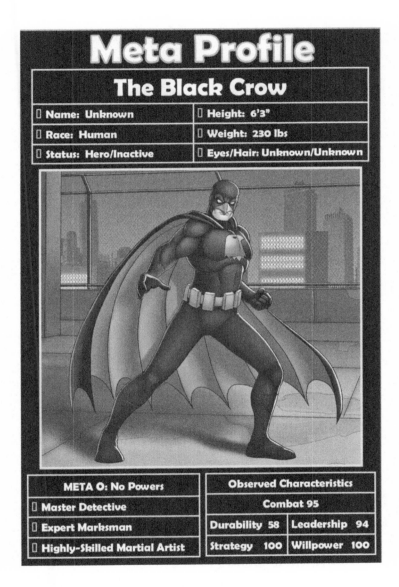

Meta Profile

The Black Crow

▢ **Name:** Unknown	▢ **Height:** 6'3"
▢ **Race:** Human	▢ **Weight:** 230 lbs
▢ **Status:** Hero/Inactive	▢ **Eyes/Hair:** Unknown/Unknown

META 0: No Powers	Observed Characteristics	
▢ Master Detective	Combat 95	
▢ Expert Marksman	Durability 58	Leadership 94
▢ Highly-Skilled Martial Artist	Strategy 100	Willpower 100

SEVEN

I CONNECT THE DOTS

A red void opens over my bed.

I hit the mattress first, followed by Grace, then Selfie, Skunk Girl, and Night Owl who all use me as their personal trampoline. My stomach is sore but I'd rather have the wind knocked out of me than fight Meta-Man any day of the week. And thanks to X-Port's teleportation power, it's a miracle we even got out of there alive. I'm just glad we made it.

But as I look at everyone spread out on the floor I realize we're not all here. One of us is missing! I look up to see the void closing fast.

Hold on! What happened to—

AAARRROOOOFFFFF!!!

Just then, a large brown-and-black rump drops out

of the void and SLAMS into my face, knocking me back on to my pillow. Ow! My nose is killing me. Just then, I see three German Shepherds standing over me licking my face. It's only after I blink a few times that they merge into one. Gee, thanks, Dog-Gone.

"Yeah, I'm happy to see you too," I say, scratching his head. "But next time look out for where you're landing."

"Are you okay, Epic?" Selfie asks.

"Just dandy," I say, rubbing my sore nose.

"Where are we?" Skunk Girl asks, looking around. "And why are Batman posters plastered all over the walls? And is that a pair of smiley-face underwear on that chair? Like, totally gross."

"Oh, will you look at that?" I say, springing from the bed and stuffing my underwear into the laundry basket. "We're, um, in my bedroom, back on the Waystation. It was the safest place I could think of to teleport to, but I wasn't exactly expecting company before I left."

"Don't worry about it," Selfie says. "You saved our bacon. That Meta-Man is one major Meta. I barely managed to grab my phone before you got us out of there. Luckily, it still works but it's still smoking from that jerk's eye beams." She holds up her magic phone which has a faint, red haze coming off of it.

"Um, what's going on?" Grace asks, sitting up and rubbing her eyes. "I feel like I missed a few chapters."

"I'm glad you're okay," I say, "but do you seriously

not remember? You tried to take down Meta-Man and he knocked your Freedom Flyer out of the sky. Then, you got taken hostage, which by the way seems to happen way too often. Thankfully, you were saved yet again."

"Oh, wow," Grace says, scratching her head. "I don't remember any of that. Well, I might as well thank you now for saving me so you don't hold it over my head for the rest of my life."

"Oh, no worries," I say with a big smile. "You don't have to thank me because I didn't save you this time."

"You didn't?" Grace says with a puzzled expression on her face. "Then who—"

BEEP! BEEP! BEEP!

Suddenly, my transmitter watch goes off, as do the watches of the rest of Next Gen.

"What's that annoying sound?" Grace says, plugging her ears.

"It's our transmitters," Selfie says, looking at her wrist. "It's a message from Pinball. He says he's in a strange country and people are yelling at him in a foreign language."

"What a surprise," Skunk Girl says, rolling her eyes. "Other countries find him just as annoying as we do."

"Wait, there's more," Night Owl says, looking at her watch. "He says he crashed into some tower that's now leaning at an angle. But he swears he didn't do it."

"At an angle?" Skunk Girl says. "That idiot! He must have smacked into the Leaning Tower of Pisa. That means Meta-Man knocked him all the way to Italy!"

"It's a good thing Pinball is pretty indestructible when he's inflated," Selfie says. "But now we've got to get him back."

"Do we?" Skunk Girl says. "Well, I'm not going."

"You won't have to," I say. "I think Glory Girl should pick him up."

"Me?" Grace says. "Why me?"

"Because Pinball saved your life," I say. "So, I'd say you owe him one."

"What?" Grace says, her eyebrows rising in disbelief. "P-Pinball saved me? Are you kidding me?"

"Nope," I say. "He took on Meta-Man all by himself. He told Meta-Man that no one messes with his girl."

"His. Girl?" Grace says, horrified.

"He's got such a crush on you," Selfie says. "Isn't it cute?"

"I think I just threw-up in my mouth," Grace says.

"Well, you can chew on that while you pick up your boyfriend in Italy," I say. "Remember, you owe him one."

"He's NOT my boyfriend," Grace says, her face turning so red it looks like her head is about to explode. And then she stands up and says, "Fine! I'll pick him up. But then we're even."

"Great," I say. "Oh, by the way, I hear Italy is quite romantic at this time of year."

"Shut it!" Grace snaps before heading for the door. But before she disappears she turns and says, "And I'm bringing earplugs!" Then, she's gone.

"Well, that's gonna be a disaster," Skunk Girl says.

Speaking of disasters, it's not like we can just sit around waiting for the next bad thing to happen. Meta-Man is still out there, and I still don't know anything about Max Mayhem. It's time to see what I can find out.

"Where are you going?" Selfie calls out.

"To the Mission Room," I yell back. "Follow me."

We race through the halls until we reach our destination. I hop into the command chair and pull myself up to the console. That's when I realize my left hand is sitting in something sticky.

"Yuck," Night Owl says. "What's that?"

"Grape jelly," I say, looking at the purple glop on my palm. "I guess Glory Girl was sucking down a jelly doughnut before she got the call from Lockdown. Does anyone see a nap—"

Suddenly, Dog-Gone's head pops up and he licks my hand clean.

"Scratch the napkin," I say, wiping the slobber off on my cape. "Now, let's see what we can find out about Max Mayhem." I punch a few commands into the keyboard and the computer does its thing. Unfortunately, the internet didn't exist when the Protectors of the Planet were fighting crime, so I'm not exactly expecting to find a listing on Wikipedia.

"Do you think you'll find anything?" Skunk Girl asks. "I mean, that guy must be ancient by now."

"I hope so," I say. "I'm tapping into the Keystone City Police Archives. If there's an arrest record for a person named Max Mayhem, it'll show up there."

Reams of data scroll down the screen until it stops suddenly. Okay, here we go. But then the computer spits back: NO RESULTS FOUND.

Ugh. Strike one.

"Well, that's not good," Night Owl says.

"Don't panic," I say. "That was just one database. Let's look at cemetery records next."

"Cemetery records?" Selfie says. "You mean, like, dead people?"

"Yep," I say, typing more commands into the computer. "Skunk Girl said he'd have to be ancient by now. Maybe he's dead. Maybe there's a cemetery plot registered in his name."

The computer goes to work and then flashes: NO RESULTS FOUND.

Strike two. Well, this is frustrating. I tap my fingers on the keyboard. Those were my two best bets and they produced absolutely nothing. Now what?

"Maybe Max Mayhem doesn't really exist," Skunk Girl says. "Did anyone think of that? Maybe he's just some fictional story character Meta-Man made up in his head. He is certifiably crazy, right?"

"Hey, that's a good one," Selfie says.

"See," Skunk Girl says, buffing her nails. "You should listen to me more often. I know crazy when I see crazy. And not just when I look in the mirror."

"No, I mean about stories," Selfie says. "How about old newspaper articles? Back then, that was the way people got their news. Reporters we're always chasing the next big story. Maybe there are articles about Max Mayhem."

"That's a great idea," I say.

"Wait, now she's getting credit for my idea?" Skunk Girl huffs.

"Chill," I say, typing into the keyboard. "We have access to the Keystone City Observer's archives. That newspaper has been around forever. We can enter a keyword and search their whole library of articles. Let's type in 'Max Mayhem' and see if we get anything."

The hourglass icon spirals on the monitor for a few seconds, and then hundreds of hits start popping up! Bingo! But as I scan the list, all of the dates are super old. Apparently, there hasn't been any news about Max Mayhem for decades.

"What about that one?" Selfie says, pointing at the last entry on the screen. "That looks intriguing."

"Protectors of the Planet Disband after Confrontation with Max Mayhem, written by Johnny Oldeson," I say, reading the headline out loud. "Yeah, that does sound interesting. Let's click it."

I select it and an article appears on the screen. Right beneath the headline is a black-and-white picture of a bald guy with a handlebar mustache being led away in handcuffs. Other than his crazy eyes, he doesn't look particularly dangerous. The caption beneath the picture reads: MAX MAYHEM APPREHENDED BY PROTECTORS OF THE PLANET.

"That's Max Mayhem?" Skunk Girl says. "Wow! He looks more like a dentist than a criminal mastermind."

"Totally," I say. "Let's see what happened."

I scroll down to the text, which reads:

Today marks the end of an era. Today, the Protectors of the Planet disbanded after a battle with the evil genius known as Max Mayhem spiraled out of control, resulting in the tragic death of our very own ace reporter, Susan Strong. Details of the confrontation are still coming to light, but what is known is that Meta-Man narrowly saved Century City from being wiped off the map.

According to credible sources, Max Mayhem, the self-proclaimed smartest person in the world, had been baiting Meta-Man, the Emerald Enforcer, for months before unleashing his devious plan. Max Mayhem held Ms. Strong hostage and attacked Century City with a horde of giant-sized robots, resulting in a cataclysmic battle with Meta-Man directly over the bustling city. Using his vast power, Meta-Man was on the cusp of victory until something went wrong and Max Mayhem fired a deadly nuclear missile into the heart of Century City. Meta-Man managed to dispatch the missile seconds before impact, but he was unable to save the life of Ms. Strong, who fell over one thousand feet to her death.

The Protectors of the Planet arrived on the scene soon after and apprehended Max Mayhem, but they were too late to save Ms. Strong. Immediately following the battle, Meta-Man was seen arguing with members of the Protectors of the Planet before flying off into the sky. In a brief statement made to the public, the Black Crow said, "The Protectors of the Planet have decided to go our separate ways. From this point forward, the Protectors of the Planet are no more."

After his shocking statement, the Black Crow did not take questions and the remaining members of the team left the scene. As the Black Crow and Sparrow shepherded Max Mayhem away in handcuffs, this reporter was able to ask Sparrow, also known as the Boy Marvel, for his take on the matter. To which Sparrow replied, "To be successful as a team, everyone has to work together in harmony. And we're no longer harmonious."

It is indeed a sad day. The Protectors of the Planet were the defenders of the innocent. Without their strong arm of justice, what will happen when the next scourge of evil inevitably appears on the scene? Who will rise to protect us?

This reporter would also like to take a moment to honor the life of Susan Strong. Ms. Strong was a seasoned, intrepid reporter who would stop at nothing to bring us the truth, even at her own personal risk. Ms. Strong worked for the Keystone City Observer for over fifteen years and served as a mentor for many young, scrappy reporters, including yours truly. Her insight and skill were a daily gift to us all, and her guts and wit will be sorely missed.

On a final note, no one has seen Meta-Man since.

After we stop reading, there's silence.

"Wow," Selfie says finally. "I mean, I think I read about a nuclear missile almost destroying Century City in my history class, but I never knew what really happened."

"Yeah," I say, "me neither."

But something doesn't feel right.

"Well," Night Owl says, "the article said the Black Crow and Sparrow took that Max Mayhem guy somewhere. Clearly, they didn't take him to Lockdown. So, where did they take him?"

The Black Crow and Sparrow.

I reread the section about the Black Crow and Sparrow.

And then my eyes focus on Sparrow's words: *"To be successful as a team, everyone has to work together in harmony."*

Where have I heard those words before?

Suddenly, a chill runs down my spine. That's when I realize Shadow Hawk just uttered those exact same words to me. But it must be a coincidence, right?

Then, I connect the dots.

Shadow Hawk.

Sparrow.

Two Meta 0 heroes named after birds.

OMG!

No wonder Shadow Hawk didn't mention Sparrow when he was rattling off members of the Protectors he was trying to find.

Shadow Hawk *was* Sparrow!

Meta Profile

Sparrow

Name: Unknown	Height: 5'4"
Race: Human	Weight: 140 lbs
Status: Hero/Unknown	Eyes/Hair: Unknown/Blonde

META 0: No Powers	Observed Characteristics	
Skilled Detective	Combat 82	
Skilled Marksman	Durability 32	Leadership 80
Skilled Martial Artist	Strategy 81	Willpower 90

EIGHT

I HAVE SOME UPS AND DOWNS

I'm kind of stunned right now.

Yet, the more I think about it, the more it makes perfect sense. Shadow Hawk must have been Sparrow when he was a kid. That's why he went off to find all of the living members of the Protectors of the Planet except for Sparrow. I mean, of course, he wouldn't need to find Sparrow—he *was* Sparrow!

And as I run through everything that's happened it all falls into place. First, neither Sparrow nor Shadow Hawk has Meta powers. Second, Shadow Hawk knows a ton of detail about the Protectors of the Planet, including the name of Warrior Woman's husband! And third, I just read an old quote from Sparrow that matches dead on with something he just said to me.

Coincidence? I'm thinking a big fat 'no.'

While Shadow Hawk is one of my all-time favorite heroes, he's also a huge mystery. I mean, even my parents don't know his true identity, and I've never seen him without his mask on. But now I've uncovered a big piece of his secret past. Shadow Hawk was Sparrow, which means he was a member of the Protectors of the Planet long before he joined the Freedom Force.

And according to that article we just read, the Black Crow and Sparrow carted Max Mayhem off in handcuffs after the battle in Century City. Which means Shadow Hawk must know what happened to Max Mayhem! I need to get in touch with Shadow Hawk as soon as possible, but all I have right now is a hunch. It would be great to show him some hard evidence so he can't deny what I'm saying.

But what can I get for evidence?

I tap my fingers on the keyboard when a light bulb goes off! I've got it! I start typing frantically.

"What are you doing?" Selfie asks, looking up at the monitor as I pull up some files.

"Checking something out," I say.

I debate telling them about Shadow Hawk being Sparrow but I want to be sure. So, with a dangerous Meta-Man flying around I'm going to have to look under every possible rock—and inside every possible database.

After a few clicks, I'm in the master network. Every member of the Freedom Force has their own private server, so I'm thinking if I can crack into Shadow Hawk's server I might find something useful. I quickly locate his folder and open it up, only to find the dreaded words: ENTER PASSWORD.

"Are you hacking into someone's account?" Skunk Girl asks. "Cool, this is like a spy movie!"

"Just let me think here," I say. Now, what would Shadow Hawk use as a password?

"Try 'swordfish,'" Skunk Girl says. "That's the password they always use in spy movies."

I try to tune her out so I can focus. Unfortunately, I barely know anything about Shadow Hawk. Caped crusading would be a whole lot easier if everything wasn't password protected.

Wait a second. Protected? Could it be?

I type in 'PROTECTORS' and hit enter. Fortunately, the password field is encrypted so the rest of the team can't see what letters I'm typing. But the screen reads: INCORRECT PASSWORD. PLEASE TRY AGAIN.

This time I type 'PROTECTORSOFTHEPLANET' and hit enter. The screen reads: INCORRECT PASSWORD. PLEASE TRY AGAIN.

Ugh!

"It's 'swordfish,'" Skunk Girl says. "I'm telling you."

"It's not 'swordfish,'" I say. "It's going to be something more specific. Something more personal. Something like—Holy cow, I've got it!"

I type 'SPARROW' and hit enter. The screen reads:

INCORRECT PASSWORD. PLEASE TRY AGAIN.

"Well, this is a bust," Night Owl says. "Let's fly."

Wait, fly? Of course. I type in 'BLACK CROWANDSPARROW' and hit enter. This time the password field disappears and I'm in!

"You did it!" Selfie exclaims.

The desktop opens and there are two file folders on the screen. One is labeled 'FREEDOM FORCE,' and the other is labeled 'PROTECTORS.' Jackpot!

"Now what?" Selfie asks.

"Now we dig further," I say.

I open the PROTECTORS folder, and to my surprise, there's only one file inside. I click it open to find a spreadsheet with only three lines on it:

BLAIR MANOR

LEVEL 13

CODE: MM69244AE7X

"Um, what does all of that mean?" Night Owl asks.

"And what's Blair Manor?" Skunk Girl asks.

"Wait, I think I've heard of Blair Manor," Selfie says. "Isn't Blair Manor that rundown mansion on the outskirts of town? I remember reading about it in the local paper. The city was going to knock it down because the owner hadn't paid taxes on the property in years. But then some anonymous donor stepped in and paid it all up, saving the manor at the last minute. It was a big story for a few weeks."

"Okay," Night Owl says, "but what is that code for?

The front gate?"

"I don't know," I say, "but we're about to find out."

***

It's dark by the time we reach Blair Manor. This time I left Dog-Gone behind and he wasn't happy about it. But even though he has the perfect power for a covert mission like this, stealth isn't exactly his strong suit—especially if he spots a small critter.

At least Grace and Pinball will be back soon to keep an eye on him. That is, unless Grace ejected Pinball from her Freedom Ferry. But as likely as that scenario seems, I can't worry about it now because we've got more important things to figure out. Like, for instance, what's on the thirteenth floor of Blair Manor?

I managed to do a little research on the way over and learned that Blair Manor belongs to someone named Bennett Blair, a billionaire who owned a big corporation before it went bankrupt. I didn't have time to find out what happened to him, but as we approach Blair Manor I figure it can't be good because the place looks like it should be condemned.

Black, twisty vines cling to the home's exterior, threatening to swallow it whole, the over-sized windows are either broken or covered in grime, and the towers bookending the manor are so crumbly they look like they'll fall down if you so much as sneeze. And just to add to the eerie ambiance, there isn't a single light on across the entire estate. So, in short, I'd say the place looks way more 'haunted' than 'house.'

"Well, this is disturbingly spooky," Skunk Girl says.

"Spooky or not," I say, "I've got to get in there."

"*You?*" Selfie says. "What about us?"

"You guys should stay here," I say. "It's too risky for all of us to go inside. We don't want to get caught. I can ride one of Night Owl's shadow slides to that busted window on the top floor and slip right in."

"Now there's a plan I can get behind, boss-man," Skunk Girl says, punching me in the arm. "You're right, there's no need for all of us to go inside that incredibly scary, super-creepy, I'll-have-nightmares-for-days house. We'll just wait out here."

"Well, I'm coming with you," Selfie says, crossing her arms. "It's too dangerous for you to go alone."

"I don't think that's such a good—," I start.

"I'm coming and that's final," Selfie says firmly, ending all debate. "Night Owl, give us a lift."

"Right," I say. Well, maybe it wouldn't be so bad to have some company.

"All aboard," Night Owl says, creating a shadow slide by our feet.

I step on first and then Selfie follows. But as soon as she puts her hands on my shoulders I feel butterflies in my stomach. Okay, get it together, Elliott. You've got to concentrate here.

"Wind us around those tall hedges and then lift us fast so no one sees us," I say to Night Owl.

"Roger," she says. Then, the shadow slide takes off.

"Try not to die!" Skunk Girl offers helpfully.

"Hang on!" I call back to Selfie as we snake our way through the overgrown garden. But the closer we get, the more I realize the window isn't as large as I thought it was. In fact, it looks like it's going to be a tight squeeze.

We're at the base of the manor in no time and then we're suddenly going straight up! Now, I'm no physics expert, but as we hurtle towards the window it dawns on me that when this slide comes to a full stop we're going to go flying like nobody's business. I peer over my shoulder to get Night Owl's attention but I can't even see her anymore. So, this is going to go one of two ways— survival or splat! I can't let Selfie get hurt!

"Get in front of me," I say, spinning Selfie around my body just as we reach the window. "Now jump!"

Just then, the shadow slide stops short and Selfie leaps forward, disappearing through the window. I lift my arms and dive in behind her, amazed that we made it until my feet catch the windowsill and I land hard on my stomach, knocking the wind out of me.

"Are you okay?" Selfie whispers, kneeling over me.

No, but I'm not going to tell her that. So, I force a fake smile and give her a thumbs up.

"Well, thanks for putting me first," she says. "I appreciate it."

"N-No problem," I say, trying to catch my breath. "Just… need a sec. Or… maybe five." Note to self: Talk to Night Owl later about power control.

"I think we're in a library," Selfie whispers.

I finally get to my feet and look around. It's dark in here, but there's enough moonlight coming through the window to make out the rows of bookshelves lining the walls. I take the flashlight out of my utility belt and shine it around. That's when I notice layers of dust on the tables and cobwebs covering the chairs. It's like no one has been in here for years.

"The light switch doesn't work," Selfie whispers, flicking it on and off. "There's no power."

"Interesting," I whisper. "Let's keep moving."

But then I realize something and shine my light at the ceiling.

"What's up?" Selfie whispers.

"How many stories high is this manor?" I ask.

"I counted four," Selfie says.

"Right," I say. "But that file we found said 'Level 13.' So, if we're already on the top floor how can that be?"

"I don't know," Selfie says. "That is odd. Maybe we're in the wrong place?"

"Maybe," I say. "But I don't think so."

We exit the library into a wide hallway with marble floors. We pass by several gigantic paintings and some marble busts of people I don't recognize. Well, this place definitely reeks of old money. As we continue onward, I shine my flashlight into several dark bedrooms and bathrooms but there's nothing out of the ordinary.

Then, something catches my eye.

There's an elevator in the middle of the hallway. Well, that's a convenient thing to have. I randomly push the button, and to my surprise, it lights up. Then, I hear the HUM of the elevator as it makes its way up to our floor.

"If there's no power," Selfie whispers, "then how is the elevator working?"

"Great question," I say, scratching my chin. "Be ready for anything."

DING! But when the elevator doors open, we're staring into an empty, wood-paneled elevator car. That's when I notice something else.

"The lights are operating inside the car," I say, turning off my flashlight. "For some reason, someone is maintaining this elevator service but ignoring the rest of the manor."

I glance at Selfie and then step inside.

"What are you doing?" she says.

"Checking it out," I say. I look around but there's nothing unusual except for the control panel which looks really old. There are buttons for levels 1, 2, 3, and 4, but no button for level 13. I hate to admit it, but maybe Selfie was right. Maybe we are in the wrong place.

"See anything?" Selfie asks.

"Nope," I say, studying the control panel.

"Nothing."

"Well, maybe you should get out of there," Selfie says. "Before something bad happens."

I've got to be missing something. I mean, it's not like Shadow Hawk to write something down that serves no purpose. What am I not seeing here?

"Epic?" Selfie says. "Do you hear me?"

Okay, there's no level 13, but there is a level 1 and a level 3. I wonder if—

"Epic, can you get out of there please?"

Well, I might as well give it a shot.

I put my flashlight back in my belt and then push the buttons for levels 1 and 3 at the same time.

DING!

Suddenly, the elevator jolts, knocking me off balance.

And then the doors start closing!

I look up in time to catch Selfie's alarmed face as the doors SLAM shut between us!

"Epic!" comes Selfie's muffled cry.

"NEXT STOP, THE CROW'S NEST," comes a deep, mechanical voice that echoes inside the car.

And then the elevator drops!

Meta Profile

Goldrush

Name: Alvin Zoombroski	Height: 5'10"
Race: Human	Weight: 180 lbs
Status: Hero/Inactive	Eyes/Hair: Brown/Black

META 3: Super-Speed	Observed Characteristics	
Extreme Speed	Combat 85	
Extreme Endurance	Durability 62	Leadership 72
Extreme Reflexes	Strategy 77	Willpower 91

NINE

I LEARN A FEW THINGS

I'm trapped inside a free-falling elevator.

After my stomach drops and the feeling of sheer panic partially subsides, I think back to how I got here in the first place. I mean, I only found out about Blair Manor and the mysterious 13th level after breaking into Shadow Hawk's server. And now I'm hurtling to my death after cleverly pushing the buttons for levels 1 and 3 at the same time.

When will I learn to stop being so darn clever?

But that's not all. The doors closed so fast I left poor Selfie behind, and according to the mechanical voice that echoed through the chamber, I'm heading straight for something called the Crow's Nest.

Wait a minute! The *Crow's* Nest?

As in, the Black Crow's Nest?

Just then, there's another low HUM and the elevator starts slowing down until it comes to a controlled, gentle stop. I breathe a sigh of relief. Well, I'm not a pancake so that's good, but I have no clue what's waiting for me on the other side of these—

DING!

Before I can even get into a combat stance the doors slide open. But instead of facing a horde of bad guys, I'm staring into a vast, subterranean lair which must be thirteen levels below ground. And plastered high on the ceiling is the insignia of the Black Crow.

Well, there's no doubt about it now. This must be the Black Crow's secret headquarters. Wow, I bet nobody even knows it's down here.

I step off the elevator into the circular room. There's a raised platform in the center holding the biggest supercomputer I've ever seen. All around the perimeter are various stations including a laboratory, a tools workshop, a storage center, and a gymnasium.

I have to admit this place is pretty swanky for an underground lair. And that's when I realize something else. The lights and monitors are on, which means that someone is maintaining this space too. Yet, as my eyes dart around the room I don't see anyone else here.

I head for the platform and climb up the stairs to check out the supercomputer. It's old and looks bigger than my refrigerator. But I guess I shouldn't be too surprised because computer processors were way bigger back then. Today, the Meta Monitor operates on a microprocessor smaller than TechnocRat's little toe!

The supercomputer is certainly an interesting relic, but what's even more interesting is what's happening on its monitor. It seems to be cycling through important world landmarks, from the Washington Monument to the Sphinx. It's like it's hunting for something—or someone.

Since I'm up high, I have a pretty good vantage point of the whole place. But when I turn around my jaw hits the floor, because directly behind me, set deep in the rock wall is… a prison cell!

How did I miss that? But when I glance over to the elevator, I realize my line of sight was blocked by the stairway to the raised platform. And when I look back over at the prison cell my heart skips a beat—because someone is in there!

In fact, I can see the silhouette of a man sitting inside! Except, he's not moving. Suddenly, I feel really uncomfortable. Has he been watching me this whole time?

"Um, h-hello?" I say, my voice echoing through the chamber.

But there's no response.

I squint but can't see the man's features any clearer. My instincts tell me to jump back into that elevator and get out of here, but my curiosity is just too strong. What if it's Shadow Hawk and he's hurt? That would explain why he didn't get back to Grace. Or what if it's one of the other Protectors, like Sergeant Stretch or Goldrush?

Whoever it is, I can't just leave him down here.

But then I get a more disturbing thought. What if it's a dead body? What if it's nothing but a skeleton—the remains of someone who's been trapped down here for decades? I swallow hard. Part of me doesn't want to find out, but I need to know. So, I head down the stairs and slowly make my way over.

I grab my flashlight and aim it at the bars, when—

"It would be quite inhumane to shine that light in my eyes," comes a measured, pretentious-sounding voice.

I freeze in my tracks.

H-He's alive! Well, that's a relief. But I still can't see who it is, so I point my light off to the side and turn it on. Suddenly, I see the face of a bald man with a handlebar mustache. He's sitting in a chair with his legs crossed and his arms folded across his chest, staring back at me with a pair of intense, green eyes.

Instantly, I know who he is.

"Y-You're Max Mayhem," I stammer.

"You are correct," he says, his speech very precise. "Now if you would be so kind as to tell me with whom I am speaking?"

"I-I'm Epic Zero," I say. "I'm... a Meta hero."

"It's a pleasure to make your acquaintance, Mr. Zero," Max Mayhem says. "It's been quite a while since I last spoke with a young person in costume. A long time indeed."

"So, um, exactly how long have you been in there?" I ask. "Approximately."

"Well, as you can see I am presently without a calendar or clock," he says. "But I would estimate it to be forty years, two months, five days, twelve hours, thirty-two minutes, and five seconds. Approximately."

"Oh, wow," I say shocked. "That's a really long time. But at least you're not dead. I-I kind of thought you were dead."

"Really?" he says, his right eyebrow rising. "Well, I am afraid any reports of my death have been greatly exaggerated, for, as you can see, I am very much alive. Although I would much prefer to be alive and free. So, tell me, is that why you are here? To free me? If so, all you need to do is enter the code into the wall-mounted control panel on your left."

I look to my left and see the interface on the wall. Suddenly, I realize what Shadow Hawk's code must be for. It's the code to release Max Mayhem from prison!

"Um, no," I say. "Sorry."

"That is a shame," Max Mayhem says, letting out a sigh. "Although it is refreshing to see a new face. I have been deprived of good conversation for years. The Black Crow and I used to debate for hours until he grew old and feeble. And now his pathetic protege is the only one keeping me alive. Unfortunately, he does not have the gift of gab like his mentor. It's rather sad actually. He was such a curious and gregarious boy before becoming the jaded and sullen man he is today. Nowadays he rarely utters a word."

Jaded and Sullen? Rarely utters a word?

"Wait, are you talking about Shadow Hawk?" I ask.

"The very one," Max Mayhem says. "To tell the truth, I thought his Sparrow costume looked more heroic, but I understand how a grown man in shorts would hardly strike fear in the hearts of his opponents. Oh well, I suppose it's the natural order of things. Everything evolves over time."

Well, there it is. That's all the confirmation I need that Shadow Hawk was once Sparrow. But speaking of evolving, for the first time I realize Max Mayhem looks exactly like he did in that photo taken long ago. But how is that possible? "Um, sorry to ask, but if you've been down here for forty years, why haven't you aged?"

"My, you are an observant one, aren't you?" he says, his lips curling into a sinister smile. "Let's just say I have good genes. But never mind that, why don't we talk about something more interesting, like getting me out of here. I am quite a wealthy man. Just name your price."

"Um, I'll take a raincheck on that," I say. "Besides, if I were you I wouldn't be itching to get out right now. You're probably safer right where you are."

"Whatever do you mean?" he says, his eyes narrowing. "Because if I didn't know better, I would say you're implying that I am in some sort of danger. Tell me,

Mr. Zero, has Meta-Man returned?"

His question catches me off guard.

How do I answer that?

"Well, I... I...," I stammer.

"Then, I am correct," Max Mayhem says, bounding from his seat and wrapping his long fingers around the bars. "You must release me at once. Clearly, you don't understand the danger we're all in. I am the only one who can defeat Meta-Man. I am the only one who can save the human race."

"Whoa! Slow down there," I say. "Meta-Man was a hero, just like me. You're Meta-Man's greatest nemesis. You tried to nuke Century City. I'm not letting you out of here for anything."

"A shame," he says, sitting back down. "But based on how I have been portrayed in the press, it's perfectly reasonable for you to trust him over me. After all, you do not understand why he came here in the first place."

"What are you talking about?" I ask.

"Contrary to popular belief," he says, "the origin of Meta-Man is nothing like the fictional story of 'Superman' from the comic books. Meta-Man was not sent here as the last of his kind from some dying planet. No, his purpose was far more sinister. You see, he wasn't sent here to protect Earth, he was sent here to destroy it."

"What?" I say, totally shocked. "I don't believe you."

"I am sure you don't," Max Mayhem says. "However, it is the truth. Meta-Man comes from a superior race of alien beings—a race whose sole purpose is total domination. To them, we are nothing but fleas on the cosmic skin of life. Meta-Man was programmed to eliminate us, but something went wrong on his long journey to Earth and when he arrived he believed he was a hero. But that was never his true destiny."

Max Mayhem pauses and I'm so dumbfounded I can't even find the words to reply. I mean, does he really think I'm buying this? This is probably a ploy to get me to free him. Well, sorry, I'm not that gullible.

"I think I've heard enough," I say.

"Before you pass judgment," he says, "would you like to know what really happened at Century City?"

I hesitate for a moment. I mean, I am curious about what happened, but I highly doubt his version of the story is the truth. But maybe there's something I can learn to help me find Meta-Man.

"Sure," I say. "Tell me your side of the story."

"Very well," he says, his eyes growing wide. "What happened in Century City was unfortunate, but necessary. You see, after countless years of searching, I finally discovered how to destroy Meta-Man once and for all. But, at that time, it was still only a theory. To confirm that it would work I needed to test it in practice. And to do that, I had to get Meta-Man close to me. Fortunately, I wasn't alone in recognizing the danger Meta-Man posed. By chance, one of Meta-Man's very own teammates reached out to me."

Wait, what?

"We held a meeting in secret," he continues, "where we discussed our mutual concerns about Meta-Man and his potential to dominate the human race. And unlike Superman, unless my theory was correct, there was no Kryptonite to stop him. So, together, we developed a plan to ensure the long-term survival of humanity."

"Hold up," I say. "Are you telling me you teamed up with one of the Protectors of the Planet?"

"Indeed," he says. "And that is how I learned about Meta-Man's girlfriend. A human girlfriend, no less. And once I kidnapped her, it was child's play to get an unsuspecting Meta-Man close to me."

Meta-Man had a girlfriend? But who?

And then that article from the Keystone City Observer comes back to me. Susan Strong, the reporter!

Meta-Man's girlfriend must have been Susan Strong!

"Once Meta-Man learned that I held his one true love captive," Max Mayhem continues, "he predictably came racing headlong to save her. And that is when I struck him with the secret weapon I had fashioned into an armored glove. And do you know what happened next?"

"Um, no," I say.

"He was injured!" Max Mayhem says, his voice sounding almost giddy. "I struck him right in the face, below his left eye. And that's when I knew my theory was correct! But remarkably he did not bleed. Instead, a flash of pure Meta energy left his once impenetrable body. I still remember the surprise on his face when he saw it. The terror in his eyes when he realized he wasn't immortal. And that's when we both knew I could kill him."

Suddenly, I remember seeing that scar beneath Meta-Man's left eye. That must have come from Max Mayhem!

"But… you didn't kill him," I say. "You killed Susan Strong."

"I suppose you could see it that way," Max Mayhem says. "But from my perspective, I would say Meta-Man was responsible for her death. You see, I gave him a choice, he could either save his beloved girlfriend, or he could save the citizens of Century City from my nuclear missile. I thought for sure he would save his true love, but then Ms. Strong begged him to forget about her and save the innocent. She said she would never forgive him if he let them die. So, ultimately it was his decision, wasn't it?"

"You're evil," I say.

"Perhaps," he says. "But I am also practical, and at that point, I needed to escape by whatever means necessary to carry out the rest of my plan. But be careful not to sympathize with that monster. You must remember, despite his heroic façade, Meta-Man was never one of us. It was only a matter of time before he realized his true destiny. And once he did, who would stop him?"

As much as I hate to admit it, he's got a point there.

"So, if Meta-Man has returned you need me," Max

Mayhem continues. "I am the only one who knows how to kill him."

We stare at each other when—

BEEP! BEEP! BEEP!

"What is that infernal noise?" he asks.

"My transmitter," I say, looking at my watch.

<Selfie: Epic r u ok? Where r u? Glory Girl found Shadow Hawk.>

Shadow Hawk?

"I-I've got to go," I say, backing away.

"Wait!" Max Mayhem calls out. "Release me! Don't leave me here! You need me!"

I run around the perimeter and head for the elevator.

"You have no chance!" he yells. "You will die! All of humanity will die!"

I step inside the elevator and push the 'up' button.

"Foolish child! You will—"

And his cries fade behind the closing doors.

Meta Profile

Max Mayhem

▢ Name: Unknown	▢ Height: 5'9"
▢ Race: Human	▢ Weight: 175 lbs
▢ Status: Villain/Unknown	▢ Eyes/Hair: Green/Bald

META 0: No Powers	Observed Characteristics	
▢ Brilliant Scientist	Combat 13	
▢ Unparalleled Inventor	Durability 8	Leadership 93
▢ Master Manipulator	Strategy 100	Willpower 100

TEN

I VISIT A NURSING HOME

"I still don't get why we're parked in the woods outside a nursing home," Skunk Girl says.

"Because this is where Glory Girl told us to meet her," Selfie says. Then, she turns to me and asks, "Are you okay, Epic? It sounds like that Max Mayhem guy was pretty demented."

"What?" I say, resting my head on the Freedom Ferry's dashboard. "Oh, yeah, I'm fine thanks."

Selfie smiles so I guess she believes me, but truthfully I'm far from okay.

I mean, I told the team about my encounter with Max Mayhem in the Black Crow's Nest, but I didn't tell them everything. Especially the part about Shadow Hawk being Sparrow. And Max Mayhem dropped so many other bombshells I'm still trying to process it all.

First, he told me Meta-Man wasn't sent to Earth to help humans but to destroy them. Then, he said he partnered with a member of the Protectors to get rid of Meta-Man. And that's how Max Mayhem found out that Susan Strong was Meta-Man's girlfriend, which is how he lured Meta-Man to Century City.

But there's even more to the story. Somehow, Max Mayhem figured out how to kill Meta-Man. I thought Meta-Man was indestructible, but I guess that can't be true because I saw the scar Max Mayhem inflicted on Meta-Man with my very own eyes.

Of course, I wanted to know how he did it, but I knew Max Mayhem wouldn't tell me unless I let him out of his cell. And that wasn't going to happen. So, this mystery just keeps getting more complicated and confusing.

I hear a noise overhead, and when I look into the morning sky, I see Grace's Freedom Ferry coming towards us. I don't know why she wanted to meet us here, but as she touches down I see a frown on her face and Pinball sitting next to her, talking her ears off. Well, at least she didn't eject him over the Atlantic Ocean.

But I don't see Dog-Gone. That means they must have left him on the Waystation. Boy, I sure hope there wasn't any food left out in the Galley because I'd hate to come home to that carnage. That is, if we ever get to go back home.

"Let's go," I say to my team, as Grace pops the hatch and storms out of her Freedom Ferry. "This should be interesting."

"Great to see you, Pinball," Selfie says. "You sure know how to take a licking and keep on ticking."

"Thanks," Pinball says, bouncing out of the Freedom Ferry and landing next to Grace. "I didn't know where I was, but thankfully Glory Girl came to get me. We talked the whole way back. I didn't realize we had so much in common, right Glory Girl?"

But Grace doesn't respond. Instead, she just stands there frowning with her arms crossed.

"Um, Glory Girl?" I say. "Pinball is talking to you."

"What?" she says. And then she reaches up and pulls a pair of earplugs out of her ears. "Sorry, I couldn't hear a thing."

"Well, that's embarrassing," Skunk Girl says as Pinball turns beet red.

"Anyway, we're even," Grace says to Pinball. And then she looks over at the building and says, "Now on to business. I'm pretty sure Shadow Hawk is in there. After I reached out a hundred times, he finally sent me an encrypted message telling me he was fine. So, I booted up TechnocRat's encrypto-tracker app and ran it over and over until it finally located Shadow Hawk's signal. And it came from inside that building."

I look over at the picturesque nursing home sitting atop a hill with a well-manicured lawn and beautiful gardens. A perfectly smooth driveway curves gently towards the red brick building with a sign that reads: Shady View Nursing Home. 3290 Shady View Lane.

It certainly looks like a nice place to ride out your golden years, except Shadow Hawk is way too young to be living there.

"That's a nursing home?" Pinball asks. "It looks more like a college campus."

"Yeah, a college campus full of old people," Skunk Girl says. "Bingo on the quad, anyone?"

"Don't be disrespectful," Selfie says. "They're called seniors, not old people."

"Seniors, old people, whatever," Skunk Girl says. "Why are we chasing Shadow Hawk when that Meta-Man guy is out there?"

"Don't be dense, Skunkers," Grace says, rolling her eyes. "We're here to get to the bottom of whatever is going on, and I think Shadow Hawk knows more than he's letting on."

If only she knew. I mean, I haven't even told her the half of it yet. But I feel like I still need to keep some things to myself until I talk to Shadow Hawk.

"So, what's he doing in there?" Night Owl asks.

Great question. Like Selfie said, nursing homes are for older... Wait a second! Suddenly, Max Mayhem's words pop into my head: *The Black Crow and I used to debate for hours until he grew old and feeble.*

O. M. G!

"Um, I think I know exactly what Shadow Hawk is doing here," I blurt out. "Does Shady View have a list of residents somewhere?"

"We could go inside and ask for one," Pinball says.

"No, you can't, knucklehead," Skunk Girl says. "That information is private."

Just then, I see a postal truck heading down the driveway. "But mailing addresses are usually public," I blurt out. "Hang on. I've got an idea."

I hop back into my Freedom Ferry and turn on the computer. Then, I enter a query to find the names of everyone with a mailing address of 3290 Shady View Lane. Suddenly, a huge list scrolls down my screen. But I'm looking for one name in particular so I sort the list alphabetically.

"Hello?" Night Owl calls out. "You okay up there?"

"Just give me a second," I say, looking for all last names that start with the letter B.

I scroll and scroll and then—there it is!

BLAIR, BENNETT.

That's the Black Crow's real name! The Black Crow lives inside this nursing home. That's got to be why Shadow Hawk is here. Now, I've just got to give the team the good news without revealing that Shadow Hawk was Sparrow. I hop out of the Freedom Ferry.

"Well?" Selfie says.

"Okay, here's the deal," I say. "When I was with Max Mayhem, he confirmed that the Black Crow's secret identity is Bennett Blair, the owner of Blair Manor. And I've just confirmed there's a Bennett Blair inside this nursing home. So, I'm guessing Shadow Hawk is here to take him into hiding before Meta-Man finds him."

"That makes sense," Night Owl says. "But how did Shadow Hawk find out the Black Crow's real identity?"

Uh-oh. How am I going to answer that without tipping my hand?

"Well," I say, "Shadow Hawk is the world's greatest detective, isn't he? Anyway, enough standing around. I bet if we go inside and find Bennett Blair, we'll also find Shadow Hawk."

"And some breakfast," Pinball says, holding his stomach. "I hate skipping breakfast."

We race down the driveway, past a few seniors out for a morning stroll, and into the nursing home. The lobby is nicely decorated, with blue, wall-to-wall carpet, plush sofas, and a giant bulletin board filled with activities. There's a welcome desk in the middle of the room with a friendly-looking woman sitting behind it.

Okay, I should probably take charge.

"I've got this," I tell the team. Then, I walk up confidently and rest my elbows on the desk. There's a small nameplate on top that reads: *Margie Kinford, Administration.* Okay, time to lay on the charm. "Hello, Margie, we're here to see a resident named Bennett Blair. Would you be so kind as to tell us his room number?"

"Visiting hours don't start until nine," Margie says,

looking us up and down. "And aren't you kids a little early for Halloween?"

What? And then I realize she's talking about our costumes. I'm so used to them I sometimes forget I'm even wearing one. "Good one," I say, "but that's the thing, see we're here to, um, surprise him. You see, we're, uh, we're here to deliver a singing telegram. Yes, a singing telegram! Maybe you've heard of us? 1-800-Arm-Strong-Songs?" Then, I flex my right arm and flash a cheesy smile.

"Is this really happening right now?" Skunk Girl says, smacking her palm against her forehead.

"Uh-huh," Margie says, raising her eyebrows. "Come back at nine. And maybe you want to pick up a little deodorant beforehand." Then, she takes a sip of coffee.

I look at the clock on the wall behind her which reads 6:12 a.m. That's like, three hours from now.

"B-But..." I stammer.

"Excuse me, Ms. Kinford," Selfie says, stepping forward with her phone. "Do you mind if I get a picture of you two?" Then, she looks at me with dead eyes and says, "It'll be perfect for our marketing materials."

"Sure, dear," Margie says, fluffing her hair. "Then will you kids leave me alone? This is a nursing home, not a nursery school."

"Of course," Selfie says. "If you two can just squeeze in a little closer. Great, now look at my phone."

I lean in and close my eyes as Selfie's phone flashes,

and when I turn around, Margie's eyes are glazed over.

"Now, Ms. Kinford," Selfie says, "which room was Mr. Blair in again?"

"Sixth floor," Margie says robotically, "room 622."

"Perfect," Selfie says. "You have a nice day. Oh, and by the way, you never saw us, right?"

"I never saw you," Margie repeats.

"Come on," Selfie says, as we follow her through the lobby to the elevator bank.

"Nice job 'handling it,'" Grace says, jabbing me with her elbow.

Okay, that didn't go so well, but we still got through.

One of the elevators opens and we step inside.

"Excuse me," Pinball says, stepping into the elevator last, his girth pushing the rest of us hard against the walls.

"It's... a... good thing... you skipped breakfast," Skunk Girl sputters, nearly out of breath.

"This... is... the last time... I... hang out with you idiots," Grace mutters to me, her left cheek pressed against the wall.

As the elevator climbs, I somehow manage not to pass out. Finally, there's a DING, and when the doors open Pinball gets out relieving all the pressure.

"Well, that was uncomfortable," Night Owl says, straightening her cape. "Now, where's room 622?"

"This way," Selfie says, reading a sign opposite the elevator bank.

We follow her down a large hallway and past an

empty nurse's station. There's a cup of coffee on the counter but fortunately, no one is around. As we head down the hall I look through the door windows at all the elderly people resting in their beds.

"Here we are," Selfie says. "Room 622." Then, she looks through the window and gasps.

"What is it?" I ask.

"Look for yourself," she says, stepping back.

I look inside to find an elderly man lying on his bed—and sitting beside him is a costumed man in a dark cowl. It's Shadow Hawk! So, that man must be Bennett Blair—the Black Crow! I desperately need to talk to Shadow Hawk alone and this might be my only chance.

"I've got this," I tell the team.

"Does that mean we're about to sing?" Pinball asks. "Because I'm not a very good singer."

"Um, no," I say. "Just wait here for a minute. I need to talk to Shadow Hawk."

"No dice," Grace says, pushing forward. "I've got a few choice words for Mr. Shadow Hawk myself."

"Please," I say, looking her straight in the eyes, "just give me a few minutes."

We stare at each other before she finally says, "Two minutes, and then I'm barging in."

"Great," I say. "That's all I need." Then, I open the door, step inside, and close it behind me. Shadow Hawk has his back to me and he's leaning over, his head in his hands. If I didn't know better I'd say he's upset.

"What's up, kid," Shadow Hawk says suddenly, startling me.

"H-How did you know it was me?" I ask.

"You have a certain way of shuffling your feet," he says. "Besides, it was pretty hard not to hear all of you talking outside the door."

"Right," I say, walking over to the foot of the bed and looking at Bennett Blair for the first time. His eyes are closed, his breathing is strained, and his body is hooked up to all sorts of machines. Even though he's an older man now, I can tell by his size that he was once a pretty big guy.

Then, I look over at Shadow Hawk who is just sitting there with his head down. I can't even imagine the pain he's going through seeing his old crime-fighting partner like this. I feel like this isn't exactly the best time to ask him about his days with the Protectors, but we're running out of time. So, I just go for it.

"Why didn't you tell me you were Sparrow?" I ask.

At first, Shadow Hawk doesn't respond. In fact, he doesn't even move. But then he says, "I guess you've become a pretty good detective yourself."

"Maybe," I say, "but I just put all the clues together. That's the Black Crow, isn't it?"

"Yes," Shadow Hawk says.

"Well, I'm sorry he's not in good health," I say.

"Me too," Shadow Hawk says. "You should have seen him when he was in his prime."

"So, if this is the Black Crow," I say, "then what are you doing here? I thought you were going to hide the remaining Protectors from Meta-Man."

"I was," Shadow Hawk says, clenching his teeth. "But Meta-Man got to them first. Believe me, I'd love to take the Black Crow out of here, but these machines are the only thing keeping him alive. So, I have no choice but to stay here until Meta-Man shows up. And when he does I'm going to fight him for our lives."

I smile weakly. I mean, can Shadow Hawk really stop Meta-Man? Shadow Hawk doesn't have any powers.

"But there's something else I found out," I say. "Max Mayhem told me one of the Protectors betrayed Meta-Man."

"You found Max Mayhem, huh?" Shadow Hawk says. "Not bad, kid. I'm impressed."

"Thanks," I say. "But that's not really true, is it?"

Shadow Hawk looks up at me for a few seconds, and then—

CRASH!

The window shatters! I turn away as glass shards fly everywhere, and when I look back over my heart skips a beat because someone is standing in the window frame with his hands on his hips.

It's Meta-Man!

"Yes, Sparrow," Meta-Man says. "Tell us if it's really true. Tell us which one of the Protectors betrayed me."

Meta Profile

Susan Strong

Name: Susan Strong	Height: 5'5"
Race: Human	Weight: 135 lbs
Status: Deceased	Eyes/Hair: Brown/Red

META 0: No Powers	Observed Characteristics	
Investigative Journalist	Combat 11	
Pulitzer Prize Winner	Durability 6	Leadership 90
Strives to Report the Truth	Strategy 74	Willpower 95

ELEVEN

I FEEL DEFEATED

I can't believe it!

Meta-Man just busted into the Black Crow's room at the nursing home! And if we don't do something fast he'll kidnap the Black Crow!

"How did you find him?" Shadow Hawk asks, rising to his feet.

"Oh, that was easy," Meta-Man says. "I simply kept my Super Senses tuned in to that girl from the prison. I believe the boy called her 'Glory Girl.' I had a feeling she would be useful, so I tracked her crossing the ocean and she led me here. But I never expected to find Sparrow, the Boy Marvel, here as well. I see you're still loyal to that old, self-righteous windbag."

"I'm my own man now," Shadow Hawk says.

"We'll see about that," Meta-Man sneers.

Suddenly, the door to the room bursts open, and Grace and the others charge in.

"Ready for round two, creep?" Grace says, clenching her fists as she heads straight for Meta-Man.

"No!" Shadow Hawk barks, blocking her path with an outstretched arm. "He's mine."

"You're a fool if you think you can stop me from taking the Black Crow," Meta-Man says. "I won't rest until I find out who betrayed me to Max Mayhem. And something tells me it was your mentor. After all, he was always jealous of me, wasn't he?"

"You won't be taking anyone anywhere," Shadow Hawk says. "Not while I have this."

Then, Shadow Hawk reaches into the folds of his dark cape and pulls out a shiny, metallic glove! That's funny, I thought I'd seen all of Shadow Hawk's gadgets before, but I don't remember ever seeing that one. And as he shoves his right hand inside, I notice it's covered with strange symbols.

"I'm sure it looks familiar, doesn't it?" Shadow Hawk continues. "The Black Crow held onto it after Century City. He always thought you'd come back."

Century City? What's he talking about? But when I look at Meta-Man, I see a hint of fear flash across his face. And then my eyes land on his scar and everything comes together.

O.M.G! That glove must be the weapon Max

Mayhem used to hurt Meta-Man! And now Shadow Hawk has it!

"I remember it well," Meta-Man says calmly. "But sadly, you're still no match for me. You see, you were always a useless nuisance, weren't you? A lost little boy, following the Black Crow around like a loyal puppy dog. He may have needed your hero-worship, but the rest of us didn't. We simply tolerated you, waiting for the day when you would overstep your bounds and be crushed by some powerful Meta. But somehow, that day never came. Until now."

Then, his eyes flash with red electricity.

"Um, holy cow," Pinball mutters.

"Get out of here!" Shadow Hawk yells.

Grace and Next Gen dive out of the room as Meta-Man unloads a blast of Heat Vision right at Shadow Hawk! But Shadow Hawk stands his ground and parries it aside with the metallic glove! The beams ricochet over the Black Crow's body and slice through the opposite wall!

Wow! What's that glove made of if it can deflect Meta-Man's Heat Vision like that? But I don't exactly have time to figure it out because my skin isn't nearly as impenetrable. Unless…

I've already learned I can't negate Meta-Man's powers, but I haven't tried duplicating them yet. But before I can act, Shadow Hawk charges Meta-Man and tackles him through the window! There's a tangle of capes, and then they drop clear out of sight! I run over to the window when the door flies open again.

"Where did they go?" Grace asks.

"Out the window," I say. "Look, I think you guys should find some doctors to safely move the Black Crow to another location in case we can't take Meta-Man down."

"You guys?" Selfie says. "There you go again! You can't go out there by yourself. He'll kill you!"

Well, she's probably right about that. But I can't just leave Shadow Hawk to fight Meta-Man on his own. I mean, Shadow Hawk doesn't even have powers!

"I'll go too," Grace says. "I owe him one."

"No," I say firmly. "Like it or not, he's too powerful for you too. But I might be able to help with my powers. Look, I know you don't want to hear it, but we both know you need to take control here and get the Black Crow to safety."

"Why am I always the babysitter?" Grace asks.

"Hey!" Skunk Girl objects. "We're not babies!"

"No, you're not," I say. "But imagine if Meta-Man punched you like he punched Pinball back at Lockdown. You aren't as durable as he is."

"Good point," Skunk Girl says.

"That's why I take my meals so seriously," Pinball says, rubbing his round tummy.

I look back at Grace who looks like she's going to explode. I know she's itching for revenge against Meta-Man, but it'll have to wait. "Fine," she mutters. "But as soon as the Black Crow is safe I'm coming back."

"Yeah, I figured," I say with a smile. Then, I reach out to borrow her Flight power and jump out the window.

I hit the air and it takes a few seconds to steady myself, but I don't see Meta-Man or Shadow Hawk anywhere. I climb higher for a more panoramic view but still no luck. Where did they go?

Then, out of the corner of my eye, I see a giant tree being tossed around like a twig in the distance. That's got to be them! Shadow Hawk must have lured Meta-Man away from the nursing home and deep into the woods. I just hope I get there in time.

I turn on the jets and make a beeline towards the action. The thing is, I don't have a plan. And things never go well when I don't have a plan. But it's too late now because I spot them.

They're in a clearing surrounded by trees, and Meta-Man is swinging a large trunk right at Shadow Hawk! Shadow Hawk leaps over it gracefully and hurls a Hawk-a-rang at Meta-Man, but it simply CLANGS off his rock-hard skin. This isn't going to be easy.

"Why are you so far away?" Shadow Hawk asks, raising his gloved fist. "Are you afraid to come closer?"

"I'm not afraid of you," Meta-Man says with a sinister smile. "I'm just seeing what you can do. And in my humble opinion, you're far less skilled than your beloved mentor. But now I've tired of this game."

Uh-oh.

Just then, Meta-Man stomps down with so much force it causes a fissure in the ground, and the cracks are heading straight for Shadow Hawk! But as soon as Shadow Hawk jumps out of the way, Meta-Man swings his tree trunk like a baseball bat and SLAMS Shadow Hawk in mid-air. The glove flies off of Shadow Hawk's hand as his body goes limp, and the hero lands on the ground like a ragdoll.

"Shadow Hawk!" I call out, landing by his side. I kneel to check on him, but he's barely breathing.

"It's finally mine," Meta-Man says.

What? What's his? But when I look over, Meta-Man is holding Max Mayhem's glove! Holy cow! How could I have been so stupid? I was so worried about Shadow Hawk that I forgot to pick up the only weapon capable of stopping Meta-Man! Great going, Elliott.

"Never again," Meta-Man says, tracing his scar with his fingers. "Now, nothing can stop me." And then he rears back and throws the glove so high in the air that it disappears into the blue sky.

"No!" I yell. I've doomed us all.

"You again?" Meta-Man says, now fixing his eyes on me. "You almost tricked me last time. But that won't happen again."

"Look," I say, slowly rising to my feet. "I was trying to help you. I-I thought you were a hero. But you're no hero."

"Perhaps not from your perspective," Meta-Man says. "But I no longer lower myself to human standards. You see, while I lived among you, I tried to blend in with your kind. I believed that if I behaved like a human then maybe I would be accepted by humans. So, I did everything in my power to be like you. I went to school, I took a job, I even... loved. But there were still those who wouldn't accept me because of my alien origin, and over time I started to wonder if they were right. Despite all of the good I did, I still felt like an outsider—like I was fighting against some deeper calling from within. And the more I thought about it, the more I realized I would never be accepted by your kind. But instead, if I embraced my true purpose, then maybe I would be a true hero to those who really mattered. Those who sent me to Earth in the first place."

For a second I'm stunned. I mean, based on what he's saying, Max Mayhem was right! Meta-Man wasn't sent here to help us, he was sent here to destroy us!

"Once my teammates betrayed me," he continues, "it confirmed everything I had been thinking. If the people I fought side-by-side with didn't trust me, then I was truly alone. And that's when I left Earth to find my people. But... I never could. And then, one day in outer space, it dawned on me. Maybe I wasn't supposed to find them. Maybe they would find me once I fulfilled my destiny."

"A-and what's that?" I ask, fearing the answer.

"Why, to destroy mankind," he says matter-of-factly.

"But first, I must settle some unfinished business. I need to know which of my so-called 'friends' betrayed me. Then, I will lay waste to the human race and finally be reunited with my people."

"B-But you don't have to do that," I blurt out. "Sure, there were detractors, but mankind loved you. And you said you were in love yourself. I-I know all about her. I know about Susan Strong, and she loved you."

"Don't say her name!" Meta-Man commands, his eyes crackling with red energy.

"But she was your girlfriend," I say. "You loved her and she was human."

"I warned you!" Meta-Man says.

"NO!" comes a man's voice.

Suddenly, I freeze as red beams erupt from Meta-Man's eyes. But then, someone shoves me hard and my head SMASHES into a nearby tree.

I hear a huge explosion, and then everything...

goes...

dark...

***

"Elliott?"

W-Where am I?

"Elliott, are you okay?"

Someone is talking. Who's talking to me? Boy, my head hurts. I rub my noggin which is sore to the touch.

"Elliott?"

I blink a few times, and as my vision comes back I see a girl with blond hair and blue eyes leaning over me.

"Elliott!" she says, slapping me hard across the face.

I wince. That hurt! How come everybody always slaps me when I'm down? Do I have a slap-me-back-into-consciousness kind of face or something? And then my assailant comes into focus. It's Grace!

"W-What happened?" I ask. That's when I realize I'm lying on my back at the base of a tree.

"Meta-Man got the Black Crow!" she says. "We were loading him into an ambulance when Meta-Man swooped down and took him. We barely had time to react. After he took off, I got worried and came looking for you."

"Is anyone hurt?" I ask, sitting up.

"No, everyone is fine," she says. "Well, Pinball tried to get in the way but he's okay. What happened here? Where's Shadow Hawk?"

Shadow Hawk?

Shadow Hawk! He must have been the one who pushed me out of the way before Meta-Man's Heat Vision nailed me!

"I-I don't know," I say, looking around.

And that's when I see it.

Right where I was standing, wisps of gray smoke are dissipating in the air. That's funny, it looks like one of Shadow Hawk's smoke grenades went off. Then, I see a tree snapped in half behind it, the splintered trunk still smoldering with red energy from Meta-Man's Heat Vision. I swallow hard. That could have been me if Shadow Hawk hadn't saved me. But that's not all I see, because lying next to the fallen trunk is... a utility belt.

No!

I scramble to my feet and race over to it. But when I try to pick it up it singes my glove. That's when I notice the ground beneath my feet is completely scorched.

"Th-That's Shadow Hawk's utility belt!" Grace says, her eyes wide.

"B-But..." I stammer, "Shadow Hawk would never leave his utility belt behind. Like, ever."

What happened? Then, I look around and see scraps of his cape all over the place.

And that's when it hits me.

Suddenly, it feels like there's an anvil stuck inside my chest and I drop to my knees as tears flow from my eyes.

"E-Elliott?" Grace says, wiping her eyes as her voice cracks. "This... this can't be happening, right?"

"I-I wish it didn't happen," I stammer. "B-But Meta-Man vaporized him. Shadow Hawk is dead. And he died... saving me."

Meta Profile

The Marksman

☐ **Name:** Robin Hoover	☐ **Height:** 5'11"
☐ **Race:** Human	☐ **Weight:** 186 lbs
☐ **Status:** Hero/Inactive	☐ **Eyes/Hair:** Brown/Brown

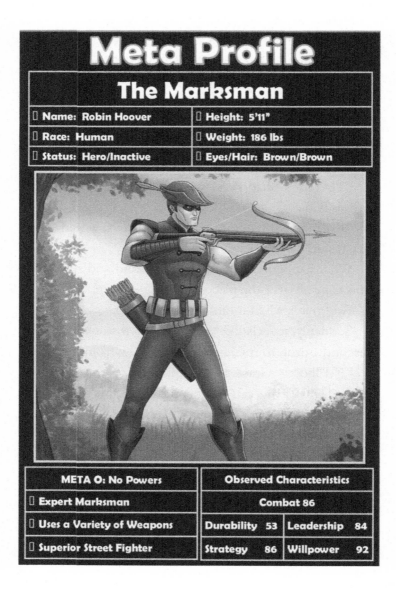

META 0: No Powers	Observed Characteristics	
☐ Expert Marksman	Combat 86	
☐ Uses a Variety of Weapons	Durability 53	Leadership 84
☐ Superior Street Fighter	Strategy 86	Willpower 92

TWELVE

I THINK I'M SEEING DOUBLE

I feel totally hopeless.

It's like someone ripped a giant hole in my heart that won't ever be mended. Shadow Hawk was my idol and now he's dead—and he died saving my life.

I can't stop thinking about all the good times we had together. The hours of one-on-one combat training, the debates over the most dangerous villain of all time, the peanut butter and banana sandwiches he'd make for me.

I-I can't believe he's gone.

And it's all my fault.

Honestly, I just want to curl up and cry, but I know that wouldn't be honoring Shadow Hawk's legacy. If Shadow Hawk were in my cape he'd soldier on. He would do whatever it takes to stop Meta-Man once and for all.

That's why I'm back at Blair Manor. That's why I'm heading down to the Black Crow's Nest to correct the mistake I made before. That's why I'm about to free Max Mayhem from prison. But this time I'm not alone.

"I can't wait to meet this nut job," Grace says.

"Just let me do the talking," I say. "You guys are here if something goes wrong."

"Gee, what could possibly go wrong?" Selfie says sarcastically. "I mean, we're only about to free the greatest evil mastermind of the Golden Age."

"Well, I'm hoping something goes wrong," Grace says, punching her hand, "because I've been itching to pop someone in the kisser."

"Relax," I say, as the elevator slows its descent. "Again, you guys are the brawn, I'm the brains."

"That's debatable," Grace mutters.

DING! The doors slide open and I'm back in the Black Crow's Nest. I think back to my first conversation with Max Mayhem and regret not bringing him along. If I had, then Shadow Hawk might still be alive today.

"Nice digs," Grace says. "It's very, um, retro?"

"This way," I say, leading them around the perimeter until we reach the prison area.

It's dark inside the cell, but I can see Max Mayhem sitting in his chair with his arms crossed.

"Is that him?" Grace whispers as we approach.

I signal for Grace and Selfie to wait off to the side as I continue to the front of his cell. Here, I can see him more clearly, and he doesn't look happy.

"I'm back," I say.

"I can see that, Mr. Zero," Max Mayhem says. "And this time you brought some friends. Am I to be the subject of a class research project?"

"Um, no," I say.

"Then perhaps you are here to provide my rations for the day?" Max Mayhem says. "Apparently, my attendant has decided not to show up for work."

His attendant? He must be referring to Shadow Hawk. Well, I'm not going to tell him what happened.

"I'm not here for that either," I say. "I'm here to offer you a deal. A deal that involves your freedom."

"My freedom?" Max Mayhem says, his left eyebrow rising. "Well, I must say this is the most excitement I've had in decades. Do tell. What is this wonderous proposal you wish to make?"

I open my mouth to speak but hesitate before any words come out. I can't believe I'm offering this, but it's not like I have a choice.

"I'll set you free," I say, "if you help me destroy Meta-Man."

"Hmmm," Max Mayhem says, tapping his pointer finger on his chin. "Let me get this straight. You are offering me my freedom in exchange for destroying Meta-Man? If I didn't know better, it sounds like you need me more than I need you. After all, we both know I am the only one capable of such a feat."

Uh-oh. I can see his wheels spinning. He's going to try pulling a fast one. I've got to stay calm and in control.

"Okay, you don't have to take it," I say quickly. "I mean, we could just leave you here if you want. And who knows when, or even if, your attendant will come back. I guess it's up to you."

"Interesting," Max Mayhem says with a crooked smile. "Are you now suggesting my attendant may never return? Things must be more dire than you had led me to believe."

Darn it! I walked into that one. I said too much and now he knows something happened to Shadow Hawk!

Way to go, Elliott.

"In that case, I propose an amendment to our little arrangement," Max Mayhem says. "I will destroy Meta-Man in exchange for my freedom. But to do so I will first require access to my secret laboratory. Being the hero that you are, I imagine you will not permit me to go there alone, so you, and only you, will accompany me as I prepare for our final battle with Meta-Man. Of course, you will be blindfolded and your friends may not track, trace, or follow us there. How does that sound?"

"Uh-uh," Grace says, stepping forward. "No way."

"Hold on," I say, putting up my hand.

"Epic, no," Selfie says. "It's too dangerous."

She may be right, but I know I can't stop Meta-Man without his help.

"You've got a deal," I say, shaking his hand through

the bars. "I'll enter the code and let you out of here, and you'll help me rid the world of Meta-Man."

***

It seems like we've been traveling for hours, and I'm pretty sure Max Mayhem doubled back a few times to throw me off the trail, but it's hard to know for sure with this blindfold on. And if anything goes wrong I'm essentially on my own because he removed my transmitter watch and insisted on taking the Black Crow's Crow-copter instead of my Freedom Ferry. Not that I blame him, of course, because part of the deal was that we couldn't be followed by Grace and Next Gen.

So, I've basically put my life in his hands.

Just. Freaking. Wonderful.

I know Grace, Selfie, and the others think I'm crazy for doing this but they weren't there when Meta-Man revealed his grand plan. The most powerful hero of all time has gone insane and if I didn't recruit Max Mayhem we'd have no shot at stopping him. I just hope this works.

As I listen to the propellers churn I think about my parents and hope they're okay. I mean, it wouldn't be the first time that wrangling a gang of villains in outer space took longer than they expected, but I sure wish I had their help. Heck, I'd even take Dog-Gone right now.

Just then, the Crow-copter seems to hover in place and I hear a loud BUZZING noise from straight ahead.

The next thing I know, the Crow-copter lurches forward, and based on the change in acoustics it seems like we're flying inside a closed space. Seconds later there's another BUZZ and it sounds like a giant door is sliding closed behind us. Suddenly, we touch down on a hard surface and I hear the propellers powering down.

"Welcome to my humble abode, Mr. Zero," Max Mayhem says, removing my blindfold.

A bright spotlight from overhead blinds me for a few seconds, but when my vision clears I'm staring into a massive hangar filled with all kinds of futuristic-looking vehicles. Then, I notice the sloped ceiling and realize we must be inside a mountain!

"Please, follow me," Max Mayhem says, as he steps out of the Crow-copter and takes a deep breath. "It is so nice to be home again."

I unbuckle myself and exit the Crow-copter. Then, I realize something. Everything in here is shiny and spotless. There isn't a speck of dust on any of the vehicles. So, if Max Mayhem has been in prison for over forty years, who's been taking care of his stuff?

"This way," Max Mayhem says, his footsteps echoing through the chamber.

I follow him through an arched doorway into a glass tube that tunnels through the mountain. After about fifty feet, the tube then connects to a four-way junction that branches off into even more glass tubes. As we walk along I kind of feel like a hamster in a plastic playset, but

I've got to admit it's pretty cool. I wonder how long it took him to build all of this.

We make a few more turns and then enter a tube that's different from the others because this one connects to a series of round, metal doors. Max Mayhem leads me to the last one and says, "This is the entrance to my laboratory. There is something inside I would like you to see."

Um, okay. Why do I have the feeling it's not his baseball card collection? He spins the wheel on the metal door, pushes it open, and then steps to the side. For a second, I hesitate as my alarm bells go off. He's not trying to stick me in a prison, is he?

"Please," he says, extending his arm. "If we are going to work together you will have to trust me."

Well, I wouldn't trust him as far as I could throw him, but he's all I've got so I cautiously step inside. As soon as I enter, my eyes grow wide with astonishment because I'm standing in the largest laboratory I've ever seen. Everywhere I look are well-organized lab stations, from rows of giant microscopes to bays of precision lasers. The walls are covered with monitors tracking experiments in various stages of completion. It's absolutely amazing. I bet TechnocRat would give his entire stash of Camembert for a setup like this.

But then I see something else.

Only a few feet away, a bald man wearing a white lab coat is entering data into a computer. And when he turns around my jaw drops, because he looks like a dead ringer for… Max Mayhem?

"Ah, Number Two," the man says. "I see you have finally returned."

Number Two? Who the heck is Number Two?

"Yes, Number Five," Max Mayhem says suddenly. "And I see you have taken over my laboratory since I've been gone."

Number Two? Number Five? What's going on?

"Pardon me," Max Mayhem says to me. "As you may have realized by now, we are both clones of the original Max Mayhem who died many years ago."

"Although there is no hard evidence of his actual death," Number Five says.

"Wait, what?" I blurt out, looking at Number Five and then back at my Max Mayhem. "You mean, you're not the real Max Mayhem?"

"Oh, no," my Max Mayhem says, "I am not."

"So, is that why you never aged?" I ask. "Because you're a clone?"

"Yes," my Max Mayhem says. "When he created us, the original Max Mayhem was able to tinker with his own cellular biochemistry to delay the aging process. So, we do grow old over time, but at a much slower rate."

"Wow," I say, trying to process everything. But then I realize something else. "Hold on. Does that mean Max Mayhem sent you, a clone, to fight Meta-Man at Century City? Are you saying the real Max Mayhem was never even there?"

"Of course, he wasn't there," my Max Mayhem says. "The original Max Mayhem was obsessed with immortality. He would never put himself at risk."

"So, you've been in prison all these years," I say, "while the real Max Mayhem was free?"

"Oh, yes," Number Five says. "I remember all of us having a great laugh when Number Two was first apprehended. But then we quickly forgot about him. There was just so much to do."

"Well, now I am back," my Max Mayhem says firmly. "And I will also be taking back my lab. Is that clear?"

"No need to pull rank, Number Two," Number Five says, walking towards us. "Per the bylaws, it is within your rights to reclaim your lab. I will simply go do the same to Number Twelve. Now, if you will excuse me."

"Number Twelve?" I say, as Number Five exits. "Wait, are you saying there are twelve Max Mayhem's out there? Are you kidding me?"

"Do not be alarmed," my Max Mayhem says. "One side effect of cloning is that as each duplicate is produced, he holds less and less true to the original copy. Thus, while I possess nearly all of the intellectual capabilities of my originator, copies like Number Five are far inferior. As for Number Twelve, I would be shocked if he even knew his own name. Now, what I wish to show you is back here. Follow me."

My mind is still spinning, but as we move past the

area where Number Five was working, I stop short and gasp. Because on his monitor is an image of something I never thought I'd see again.

It's a picture of a gold ring.

A gold ring with a lightning bolt on its face.

Meta Profile

Will Power

☐ **Name:** Lawrence Fletcher	☐ **Height:** 5'10"
☐ **Race:** Human	☐ **Weight:** 196 lbs
☐ **Status:** Hero/Deceased	☐ **Eyes/Hair:** Brown/Blonde

META 3: Magic	Observed Characteristics		
☐ **Extreme Energy Manipulation Powered by an Alien Rock**	Combat 82		
☐ **Creates Energy Constructs in Any Shape He Can Imagine**	Durability 77	Leadership	68
	Strategy 69	Willpower	99

THIRTEEN

I DISCOVER THE TRUTH

I can't believe what I'm looking at.

I mean, what is an image of the gold Ring of Suffering doing on Max Mayhem Five's monitor? The Three Rings of Suffering are super dangerous artifacts, and each ring houses a member of the Djinn Three—the three evil genie brothers who have terrorized humanity for centuries. Once upon a time, all three rings were held safe and sound in the trophy room of the Waystation 1.0.

That is, until the Meta-Busters blew it up.

As I stare at the gold ring, I think back to my encounter with Beezle, the evil djinn inside the silver ring. I'll never forget how he intentionally twisted my words around to take Siphon's life energy. Just thinking about it makes me feel nauseous all over again.

Fortunately, I was able to use the last of the three

wishes Beezle granted me to confine him to his ring forever. Now, both the silver and bronze rings are back on the Waystation 2.0, but the gold ring is still out there somewhere. And Terrog, the djinn inside, is supposedly the most powerful of them all. So, why is Max Mayhem's clone looking for Terrog?

"Can I ask you something?" I ask Max Mayhem Two. Well, now that I know he's a clone, I figure I might as well think of him that way.

"Certainly, Mr. Zero," Max Mayhem Two says.

"Great," I say, pointing to the monitor. "Can you tell me why Number Five is looking for this ring?"

"I am not sure," Max Mayhem Two says, leaning over to study the image. "I am personally not familiar with it. However, our originator always had multiple schemes in play and would assign confidential projects to different clones for execution. I suspect he had a good reason for seeking this object, but his purpose is unknown to me. Unfortunately, Number Five is unlikely to reveal why he is seeking the object unless it will significantly advance his goal. And speaking of goals, we have a common one to destroy Meta-Man, so it's time I shared the reason for our visit with you. Now, if you would kindly follow me."

But as we move on, I can't help looking back at the image of the ring. The silver ring was dangerous enough and I couldn't imagine what would happen if the original Max Mayhem got his hands on the gold one. That is, if the original Max Mayhem is even still alive.

Max Mayhem Two leads me past vats of bubbling liquid, vials filled with white, tofu-like globules, and various other stations until we reach the back of the laboratory. That's when I do a double take because we're standing in front of the largest metal door I've ever seen. It spans the entire width of the room and goes from the floor to the ceiling. What's behind that monster?

"Impressive, isn't it?" Max Mayhem Two says proudly as he types into a small keypad mounted on the door. "Let's just say I required a substantial deterrent to keep the others away from my special project."

His special project? What could that be?

Suddenly, there's a loud VOOM that echoes through the lab and the door splits open at its center.

"This way," Max Mayhem Two offers.

I look at his grinning face, step inside, and do a double take.

It's… a spaceship?

Or, more precisely, half a spaceship.

It's about twenty feet high and shaped like a capsule, with three large, curved fins at its base and a cockpit in the center that's big enough to fit a person. Strangely, half of the ship has been stripped away and I can see the understructure that forms its skeleton. And then I notice something else. The ship's metallic panels are covered with familiar-looking shapes and symbols.

Where have I seen markings like that before?

Then, I notice a bunch of lasers stationed around the ship, and several of the ship's metallic panels are splayed out on worktables. For a second I'm confused. What the heck does a spaceship have to do with defeating Meta-Man? I mean, why is he even showing me this? But then it hits me like a ton of bricks.

I know exactly whose ship that is!

"That's Meta-Man's ship!" I blurt out. "That's the ship that brought him here as a baby, isn't it?"

"Very good, Mr. Zero," Max Mayhem Two says. "That is the very ship Meta-Man used to travel to Earth. And that ship is also the key to his destruction."

"What?" I say. "Sorry, but I don't get it."

"That is understandable," Max Mayhem Two says. "At first, I didn't either, but as I mapped out the various methods of potentially defeating Meta-Man, I always suspected the solution was somehow sitting right under my nose. And that is when I remembered his ship, and then everything became clear."

His eyes gleam with confidence but I'm still lost.

"You see," he continues, "Meta-Man was valuable cargo. If his people put him inside this ship and sent him halfway across the universe, then the material this ship is made from must be incredibly strong. After all, Meta-Man's powers were formidable even as an infant, and the ship must have been built to withstand the full force of his might, not to mention whatever else he would encounter along the way—including changing atmospheric pressure, collisions with space debris, and even possible alien attack. So, if his people designed this ship to protect him, then the material on this ship must be ..."

"...stronger than he is," I say, finishing his sentence.

I'm shocked. That's pure genius.

"Precisely," Max Mayhem Two says. "Therefore, if I could break his ship down, then I could use the material to create a weapon I could use against Meta-Man. It took decades of research, decades of testing and tweaking and testing again, but I finally had my breakthrough. I finally identified a way to reshape the material. And once I did, I had to test my theory on my subject."

Test his theory? Suddenly, I realize where I've seen those markings before.

"The glove!" I exclaim. "The glove you used in Century City was made from Meta-Man's ship! That's how you gave him that scar!"

"Yes," he says. "But unfortunately, I was unable to escape from Century City, and thus, my grand plan to destroy Meta-Man never came to fruition. But now I have my second chance."

But there's something still bothering me about his story. Something that still doesn't make sense.

"But wait," I say. "How did you find his ship in the first place? I can't imagine it was still laying where he crash-landed all those years before."

"That is none of your concern," Max Mayhem Two

says dismissively. "The point is that I have it, and now I can exploit it to its maximum potential."

"Um, okay," I say. "But how?"

"With this," he says, pressing a button on a console.

Suddenly, a large box rises out of the floor, and as the front panel slides open I see a shiny suit of armor inside. But then I realize it's no ordinary suit of armor because it's covered head-to-toe with the same strange markings as the glove and ship! At first, I'm confused, but as I look at all the parts lying around I realize the suit is made entirely from the ship's material!

Well, almost the entire suit because it's missing the right glove. And then I notice there's also a matching scabbard and sword.

"You're going to fight Meta-Man with that?" I ask. And then I notice something else. "There's no visor, so how will you see?"

"To defeat Meta-Man, I must be fully encased in the battle armor with no potential openings," he says. "Therefore, I have designed a built-in radar to guide me."

Built-in radar? That sounds cool. I look at his battle armor and realize he might actually have a fighting chance. I mean, if he injured Meta-Man with just a glove, I can only imagine what a whole suit could do. And speaking of gloves, Meta-Man chucked the original glove, so what's Max Mayhem Two going to do?

"What about the right glove?" I ask. "I saw Meta-Man hurl it into outer space."

"No worries," he says, pushing another button. "I am prepared for just such a scenario."

Then, another compartment rises out of the floor with spare parts, including right and left-handed gloves. Max Mayhem Two selects a right-handed glove and says, "I simply need to weld it on."

"Well, that's good," I say. "But what do we do when you're ready? I assume there's no Bat phone to call Meta-Man over."

"No," Max Mayhem says. "If we are going to defeat Meta-Man, we will need to employ the element of surprise. And that is where you come in."

"Me?" I say.

"Yes," he says. "We will need to draw him out in the open. That will be your role."

"So, what exactly does that mean?" I ask.

"It means that you are the bait, and I am the trap," he says. "But do not worry, Mr. Zero. I'll go over everything on our journey north."

"North?" I say. "What's north?"

"Meta-Man's old secret headquarters," Max Mayhem Two says. "We will ambush him there. But first, I must attend to this glove."

***

I hate cold weather.

So, the fact that I'm standing ankle-deep in snow in

the middle of the Arctic isn't exactly what I had in mind when Max Mayhem Two told me we'd be heading north. At least he gave me a parka to wear or I'd really be in trouble. But the longer I'm exposed to the elements, the faster I'll go from being Epic Zero to Epic Sub-Zero.

And since I don't want to turn into a popsicle, I'd better find the entrance to Meta-Man's secret headquarters fast. The thing is, Max Mayhem Two didn't exactly give me directions. He basically dropped me off in the Crow-copter and told me to look for a tunnel entrance somewhere in these snow-capped mountains.

Gee, that was helpful. Not.

Even though my teeth are chattering like crazy, I trudge over to the base of the closest mountain and start searching. But there are so many rocks I could literally be here forever. Especially if I freeze to death.

Why did Meta-Man even have an old secret headquarters in this barren, frozen wasteland? It's isolated and kind of peaceful, but the surroundings are pretty bleak. But suddenly I get it. If Meta-Man never felt human, well, no humans would ever find him here. In fact, I think the only thing alive in these parts is me.

But that probably won't last long, even if I somehow stumble across this magical entrance. After all, Max Mayhem Two's big plan is for me to go inside Meta-Man's headquarters and draw him out in the open. That's when Max Mayhem Two will take him by surprise.

I suppose it's a great plan—if you're not me.

Why did I agree to this?

Well, I'm not finding anything that looks like an opening and my fingers are starting to freeze under my gloves. I consider yelling Meta-Man's name at the top of my lungs, but the wind is whipping so hard there's no way he'd hear me. So, I'll just have to keep searching and pray for a miracle.

That's when I notice something unusual hanging overhead. There's a piece of rock sticking down that looks just like an arrow—and it's pointing at a large boulder sitting on a ledge about ten feet up. It might be nothing but that arrow-shaped rock just seems too odd to be a coincidence. I might as well check it out.

Using all of my strength, I scramble up the slippery mountain until I reach the ledge. That's when I see the boulder which is taller than me. Well, that was all for nothing. I'm about to climb back down when I notice a large hole behind it. That's weird. I lean over the snow-covered boulder for a closer look when I see an opening that leads right into the mountain itself.

That's it! It's the tunnel!

Now that's a great optical illusion because if you were looking from straight on you'd never see the entrance. Well, if I can't get Meta-Man to come out, then I guess I'll have to go in. I take a deep breath and slide down the snowy boulder into the tunnel. My backside is soaked but sometimes you've gotta do what you've gotta do.

I make my way cautiously, the tunnel growing darker with every step. I'd love to use my flashlight but I'm afraid it might give me away. And speaking of giving myself away, my heart is beating so loud it sounds like it's echoing down the tunnel. Every bone in my body tells me to turn back, but I can't let Shadow Hawk down. I need to be brave. I need to do this for him and everyone else.

After about a hundred yards, I hit a fork in the tunnel. Great, which way should I go? I'm about to deploy my fail-safe, decision-making strategy of eeny-meeny-miny-moe when I hear something faint coming from the pathway to the left. Is that... whistling? I lean in and raise my ear. Yep, someone is whistling, which means that someone is down there.

So, I turn left and follow the noise. At first, I'm not sure what tune it is, but as I get closer it kind of sounds like "Taps." I wonder who'd be whistling that?

Then, it dawns on me that it might be coming from one of the Protectors of the Planet. According to Shadow Hawk, Meta-Man had captured all of the living members. I doubt it's the Black Crow based on the state he was in at the nursing home, but it could be one of the others, like Goldrush, the Marksman, Sergeant Stretch, or Warrior Woman. Suddenly, I realize I'm walking a bit faster than I thought. I guess it's second nature now that if someone is in trouble I'll race to the rescue.

The whistling gets louder as I reach the end of the tunnel which opens into a large chamber. I hug the edge of the wall, peer around the corner, and nearly let out a loud gasp. That's because I see five older people with their limbs stretched wide and their hands and feet encased in blocks of ice!

I don't know what I was expecting, but it certainly wasn't this. I recognize the Black Crow which means the others must be his teammates. The three who resemble Goldrush, the Marksman, and Warrior Woman look semi-alert, but Sergeant Stretch and the Black Crow have their heads down.

I've got to help them! But then I realize something.

The whistling has stopped.

Why did the whistling stop?

"Please, do come in," Meta-Man says, his voice echoing through the chamber.

I pull my head back and hold my breath. Darn it! How did he know I was here? I thought I was quiet.

"Don't be shy," he says, his voice booming off the walls. "I know you're out there. I do have Super-Hearing, you know."

I curse myself under my breath. I was hoping to avoid a direct confrontation, but that'll be impossible now. So, I grit my teeth and step into the chamber. And that's when I see Meta-Man sitting on a throne of ice.

"It's about time," he says. "I was getting bored waiting for you."

"Let them go!" I demand, trying not to look scared. "They didn't do anything to you!"

"That's not true," Meta-Man says. "One of them betrayed me, but none of them will tell me who did it. I nearly got it out of Sergeant Stretch, but his weak heart gave out before he could reveal the name."

His heart? I look at Sergeant Stretch and realize he isn't breathing. Then, I see the Black Crow struggling to breathe without his medical equipment.

"You'll kill him!" I yell. "He needs help!"

"And so do you," Meta-Man says. "But you're not alone, are you?"

I keep my mouth shut. I can't let him know about Max Mayhem Two. It would ruin the element of surprise.

"So, where is my lovely father anyway?" he asks.

"Um, sorry?" I say, totally confused. "What?"

"I asked you where my father was," Meta-Man says. "I assume he put you up to this."

"What are you talking about?" I ask. "I don't know your father."

"Oh, but you do," he says. "Because my father is Max Mayhem."

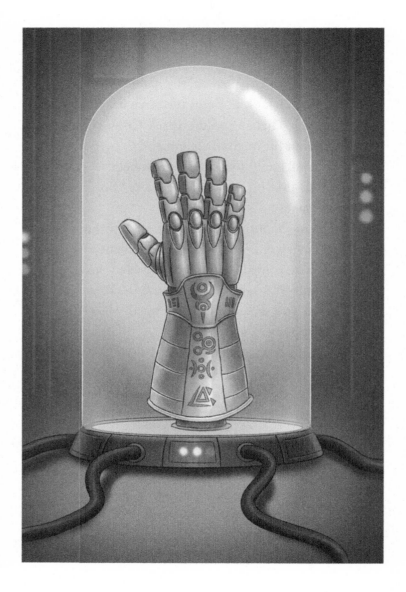

FOURTEEN

I GET MIXED UP IN A FAMILY AFFAIR

Um, what?

Did I just hear what I thought I heard? Did Meta-Man just say that Max Mayhem was his father? But that's impossible because they're arch enemies, right? I mean, the Joker wasn't Batman's father. The Green Goblin wasn't Spider-Man's father. So how could Max Mayhem be Meta-Man's father? Archenemies just aren't supposed to be related like that!

Besides, Max Mayhem couldn't be Meta-Man's father because Max Mayhem is human, while Meta-Man is an alien who adopted Earth as… his… home.

O. M. G.

Adopted?

Just then, I remember Meta-Man's profile, and one particular sentence sticks out in my mind: *His ship landed*

near Houston where it was discovered by a corrupt oil baron named
Maximillian Murdock.

Wait a second.

Maximillian Murdock?

Max Mayhem?

Maximillian. Max.

Suddenly, everything hits me at once and I feel like such a fool. Max Mayhem is Maximillian Murdock! Which means Max Mayhem is Meta-Man's adopted father! No wonder Max Mayhem had Meta-Man's ship! He simply kept it after he discovered Meta-Man!

And now he's trying to kill his son!

"He's out there, isn't he?" Meta-Man asks. "I can see it on your face. He sent you here to do his dirty work. That's so like him. But you don't have to die for him. If you tell me where he is, I'll spare your life."

I open my mouth to offer a clever retort but no words come out. Honestly, my brain is so scrambled I'm not sure what I should do right now. I mean, why didn't Max Mayhem Two tell me about this? Why didn't he tell me Meta-Man was the original Max Mayhem's son?

"D-Don't listen to him," comes a woman's voice. "He's... lying to you. He'll... kill you."

I turn to see Warrior Woman looking at me, the veins in her neck bulging as she tries to break her hands and feet free of her ice shackles, but she can't.

"Silence!" Meta-Man orders as he rises from his ice throne. "I make the rules here!"

I realize that as much as I want to help Warrior Woman and the Protectors, Meta-Man is way too powerful for me to fight on my own. I might not trust Max Mayhem Two, but he's still the best option I've got.

"So, child," Meta-Man says, stepping down from his ice platform, his eyes glowing red. "What's it going to be? Will you help me, or will you die?"

"Run!" Warrior Woman yells.

Run? Well, that's the best idea I've heard all day. Now, I may not be Blue Bolt, but luckily I'm standing near the next best thing. So, I concentrate hard and reach out to Goldrush, pulling his power into my body. And as his Super-Speed flows through my veins, I realize his Meta energy doesn't feel as strong as I had hoped, but it's way better than what I've got now.

"You make a compelling offer," I say to Meta-Man, "but I'm gonna split." Then, I take off as fast as I can, heading back through the tunnel.

I'm feeling pretty good about my getaway until I realize I'm not alone. I hear footsteps behind me, and when I peer over my shoulder Meta-Man is right on my tail! Great, I forgot he's got Super-Speed too! Even though I'm running so fast sparks are flying from my feet, he's still catching up to me! I hope I remember the way I came in!

I hang my first right and see light in the distance. Yes! This has got to be the way out! I pump my arms and legs with everything I've got until I see the giant boulder up ahead. I bound over it into the daylight and find myself flying through the air! Uh-oh, I forgot the entrance was ten feet off the ground! The next thing I know, I land hard on my stomach, catching a face-full of snow.

Awesome. Just need to… catch my breath.

"Have we reached the end so soon?" Meta-Man asks from behind me, his dark shadow eclipsing my body.

I get up on my knees and realize I'm shivering. Somehow, I've lost my parka and my costume is ripped in various places. But that's not all I notice, because Meta-Man's eyes are glowing! This is it! But then—

"Back off, Lucas!" comes a voice from overhead. Suddenly, there's a CLANG and Meta-Man goes flying backward into the mountainside.

That's when a knight in metallic, shining armor appears before me, except I know there's no noble gentleman inside. It's Max Mayhem Two! And he just clocked Meta-Man with his battle armor!

"Don't you dare call me by that name!" Meta-Man responds, getting to his feet and wiping his mouth with his sleeve. "I'm no longer your son!"

"But I will always be your father," Max Mayhem Two says. "And I will always know what's best for you. It is time we ended this, Lucas. You knew that if you ever came back I would be forced to kill you."

"Just like you killed Susan?" Meta-Man asks. "She was innocent in all of this. And yet, you disposed of her like she was nothing."

"She *was* nothing," Max Mayhem Two says. "You knew it was wrong to start a romantic relationship with a human, yet you did it anyway. You were always different, and if it took her death for you to finally accept the truth, then it was well worth the sacrifice."

"I tried to fit in!" Meta-Man yells. "I wasted my life trying to help humanity!"

"You did try," Max Mayhem Two says. "But we both knew it was all for nothing. You see, from the moment I found you I suspected you were sent here for a reason. It just wasn't apparent what that reason was. But one day, while I was transcribing an ancient text, it came to me. I realized the key to understanding you, the key to understanding everything about you, was always right in front of my eyes. Do you see these strange markings on my armor? These came from your spaceship. But they aren't just random decorations, they're words—they're the words of your people. I realized that they left a communication for you in their own language right on the exterior of your ship. And once I finally cracked the code, their message became all too clear."

"My people left a message for me on my ship?" Meta-Man says, clearly shocked. "Is that why you told me my ship was destroyed when I landed here? Because you never wanted me to see the message? Tell me! Tell me what the message said!"

"You would like that, wouldn't you?" Max Mayhem Two says. "Unfortunately, I cannot do that. But what I can share is that it wasn't so much a message as it was instructions—instructions on how you should contact your people once your mission to annihilate humanity was complete. That is why I ensured you never laid eyes on your ship."

"I can't believe you kept that from me," Meta-Man says, standing tall. "I can't believe you kept me from discovering my true identity. I'll kill you!"

"You can certainly try," Max Mayhem Two says, pulling his gleaming sword out of his scabbard.

Suddenly, there's a blur as Meta-Man uses his Super-Speed to attack Max Mayhem Two, but Max Mayhem Two stands his ground and leans in, repelling the former hero with his shoulder. Undeterred, Meta-Man picks up a huge boulder and hurls it at his father. But this time Max Mayhem Two slices it in half with his sword before it even reaches him.

Next, Meta-Man flies at Max Mayhem Two with tremendous speed but Max Mayhem Two dodges him and lands a roundhouse kick, sending Meta-Man flying into a rock wall. Holy cow! I can't believe it! Max Mayhem Two is matching Meta-Man blow for blow! He might actually do it! He might actually defeat Meta-Man!

"Must we continue?" Max Mayhem Two asks. "Surely, you can see you are no match for me and my battle armor. Why delay the inevitable? You are clearly a lost and tortured soul. As your father, let me be the one to put you out of your misery. And afterward, I promise to finish off the Protectors of the Planet in your honor."

Um, what? Finish the Protectors? Okay, now I know I can't trust that guy. The thing is, how am I supposed to beat him after he destroys Meta-Man?

"Never," Meta-Man says, flying high into the air. But instead of attacking, this time he just hovers overhead, staring down at Max Mayhem Two.

What is he doing?

"Come down and let's get this over with!" Max Mayhem Two commands, like a father berating his spoiled child. "You will not win anything from up there."

"Perhaps not," Meta-Man says with a sly smile. "But from here I can use my Super Senses to scan your battle armor. And while you've done an excellent job overall, I see you've gotten a bit rusty after all of these years."

"What?" Max Mayhem Two says with clear concern in his voice. "What are you talking about?"

"Well, it appears your attention to detail just isn't what it used to be," Meta-Man says. "Because my Super-Hearing is detecting just the slightest difference in sound as the wind blows across parts of your armor."

"No…" Max Mayhem Two says.

"Oh, yes," Meta-Man says with a big smile. "In fact, it 'seems' like there's quite a gap in the 'seam' of your right glove. And I think that's going to be a fatal mistake for you."

But before Max Mayhem Two can react, Meta-Man is a blur. And the next thing I know he's crouching beside

Max Mayhem Two, firing a pinpoint beam of Heat Vision directly into Max Mayhem Two's right wrist! Holy cow! That's where Max Mayhem Two just welded on the new glove!

"NO!" Max Mayhem Two screams, and then there's a giant IMPLOSION inside the battle armor! I shield my eyes from the light, and when I look back Max Mayhem Two's battle armor is lying face down in the snow with a trail of red smoke emanating from his right wrist.

"That was for Susan," Meta-Man says, standing up.

I-I can't believe it! Max Mayhem Two is dead! Fried inside his own suit! But I doubt Meta-Man even knows that Max Mayhem Two was a clone and not his real father.

Now what do I do? I mean, Max Mayhem Two was supposed to take care of Meta-Man. And now Meta-Man is looking at me!

"Hey," I say. "Look, I-I didn't know anything about your whole father-son thing. He never told me. But I'm sorry. It didn't sound like the best childhood a kid could have."

"It wasn't," he says. "But it's over now."

"Great," I say. "So, does that mean you're leaving now? I mean, you did what you came here to do, right? You got revenge on your father. Wasn't that enough?"

"No," Meta-Man says. "That was just the beginning."

"Um, the beginning of what?" I ask.

"The beginning of discovering my true identity," Meta-Man says. "Thanks to my 'father,' all of the pieces have now fallen into place. First, I must destroy the human race. Then, I will decode the instructions of my people and finally learn who I really am."

Meta Profile

Sergeant Stretch

⬜ Name: Patrick Johnson	⬜ Height: 6'1"
⬜ Race: Human	⬜ Weight: 202 lbs
⬜ Status: Hero/Inactive	⬜ Eyes/Hair: Brown/Black

META 3: Meta-morph	Observed Characteristics	
⬜ Extreme Body Morphing	Combat 81	
⬜ Can Stretch His Body into Various Shapes	Durability 94	Leadership 83
	Strategy 72	Willpower 82

FIFTEEN

I FIGHT FOR ALL OF HUMANITY

This is not good.

Meta-Man just destroyed Max Mayhem Two, who was not only the clone of his adopted father but also the only person capable of stopping him. And now that Max Mayhem Two is gone only one person is standing between Meta-Man and the annihilation of the human race—and that's me!

I get to my feet and try to come up with a plan. I don't feel Goldrush's Meta energy inside me anymore, and at this point, Meta-Man is way beyond reasoning with. We both know I can't negate his powers because he can sense it coming, but I haven't tried duplicating them yet.

"You will be the next to die," Meta-Man says, coming towards me, "but you will not be the last."

"Not if I have anything to say about it," I reply, and then I concentrate hard, reaching out for his power, and then pull it back to me. But as his Meta energy flows through me, I realize I don't know what power I've just copied. I mean, Meta-Man has Super-Strength, Super-Speed, Heat Vision, and Flight, but he can only use one power at a time. So, which power did I just grab?

Please, tell me it's Super-Strength!

"Farewell," Meta-Man says, rearing back to punch me into next week.

But then my instincts kick in and I strike first, punching him over a hundred times in the breadbasket with lightning-fast quickness. That's when I realize I didn't get his Super-Strength, but Super-Speed! Except, despite all of my pounding, Meta-Man doesn't budge because I'm only as strong as I am now—which isn't strong at all. Just then, pain shoots from my knuckles up my arms! Ouch! It feels like I just slammed my fist into a steel door a hundred times!

My arms are throbbing, but I still manage to dart out of the way with ease as he swings at me, punching a sizeable hole into the mountain behind me. Okay, Super-Speed is helpful, but it won't be enough to take him down.

I'm gonna have to gamble on another power.

"So, I see you can copy my powers as well," he says, wheeling on me. "Impressive. But I'll figure you out. I always do."

Suddenly, his eyes light up and I bolt just as his Heat Vision scorches the ground beneath me. Well, I'm not going to last long like this. If I can grab his Heat Vision I could try fighting him from long range. So, I concentrate and pull in his powers again.

But as I absorb his new Meta energy, I can feel his old Meta energy slipping away. Meta-Man takes off into the air and I lock my gaze on him. But when I try to activate my Heat Vision nothing happens! That's when Meta-Man circles closer and smiles.

"See, I told you I'd figure you out," he says. "You can copy my powers, but it won't help you much if I'm always one step ahead."

One step ahead? What's he talking about?

Suddenly, I realize I can hear everything around me super well, like the ruffles of his cape fluttering in the wind, the pitter-patter of snowflakes hitting the mountainside, and the drops of sweat falling from my forehead onto the snow. And that's when I realize what he's saying. He felt me using my duplication power and switched his Meta energy to the most useless combat power ever—Super Hearing!

"You might as well surrender," he says, landing in front of me. "Otherwise, I'll just keep shifting my Meta energy around to keep you off balance. You have no chance."

I swallow hard because I know he's right. I can keep trying to grab his current power, but he'll just change it to the next one. I need a different plan. The problem is, I don't know what else to do.

And that's when I hear someone breathing. Someone other than me and Meta-Man!

"Leave the boy alone!" comes a gritty, familiar voice.

I turn to see a dark figure standing on an icy boulder, and I can't believe my eyes. It's... Shadow Hawk!

"Well, well," Meta-Man says, turning to face him. "Look who survived after all. It must be my lucky day because I get to kill you all over again."

Just then, I hear footsteps behind me, and then—

"If you're going to kill him," comes a woman's voice, "then you'll have to kill us too."

I spin around to see three more familiar figures standing beneath the entrance of the tunnel. It's Warrior Woman, the Marksman, and Goldrush! Shadow Hawk must have freed them!

"It's a reunion," Meta-Man says with a sneer. "Unfortunately, I see not all of us could make it. Should I assume the Black Crow died as well? A shame. I was so looking forward to ending his life with my bare hands."

"You can't hold a candle to the Black Crow," Shadow Hawk says. "He's everything you're not. Brave. Honorable. Decent."

"Interestingly, you didn't use the word 'loyal,'" Meta-Man says. "Out of all of you, I always suspected he was the one who sold me out to Max Mayhem. He was always jealous of me. And why wouldn't he be? After all, I had the powers. The headlines. The girl."

"What are you talking about?" Shadow Hawk asks.

"Why, Susan Strong, of course," Meta-Man says. "She told me the Black Crow was interested in her, but she wanted nothing to do with him. No surprise there, of course. After all, he was a rather moody fellow. So, putting two and two together, it wouldn't surprise me in the least if he was the traitor you were protecting. And I was just about to find out when I was interrupted by this child."

"If you're looking for your traitor," Shadow Hawk says, "then look no further."

"Wait, what?" I blurt out.

"You?" Meta-Man says with a chuckle. "Do you expect me to believe that it was you who betrayed me? Nice try, but you were a boy."

"Yes, I was a boy," Shadow Hawk says. "But I was no fool. Not after I found out who you really were that day we battled Hypnotica. Or don't you remember?"

"Hypnotica?" Meta-Man says, his eyebrows rising.

"I'm not surprised you're having trouble recalling that mission," Shadow Hawk says, "so let me refresh your memory. It was our last mission before Century City, and you, me, and the Black Crow were on duty. We received a call at Protector Palace from the police commissioner that Hypnotica, the self-proclaimed Queen of Hypnosis, was robbing the Keystone City Bank. We went to stop her and while you and the Black Crow went inside the bank, I waited around back in case she escaped. But Hypnotica had set a trap, and as soon as you went inside, you were both put under her hypnotic spell. And do you remember what happened next?"

"Let me guess," Meta-Man says. "You saved the day."

"I did," Shadow Hawk says. "But that wasn't all. When I found you, you were still under her hypnotic power. At first, you started babbling gibberish. But then your words became more coherent, and you kept going on and on about your secret destiny, your one true purpose. I didn't know what you were talking about. I thought you were just joking around. So, I figured I'd just play along. But when I asked you what your destiny was, you said it was to destroy the human race."

"You never told me that," Meta-Man says.

"Of course not," Shadow Hawk says. "But do you know who I did tell? The Black Crow. And do you know what he said? He said you were probably just having a bad dream. But he wasn't there. He didn't see the anger and determination in your eyes when you were saying it. I may have been a kid, but I knew you weren't having a bad dream. I had learned all about the power of hypnosis and its ability to surface things from people's pasts they weren't even aware of themselves. I knew you were speaking your truth, and that's when I realized that if you ever decided to carry out your true purpose there wasn't anyone on Earth who could stop you. And that's when I tracked down Max Mayhem."

"So, you *are* responsible," Meta-Man whispers, his eyes narrowing. "You're responsible for Susan's death."

"Her death is my greatest regret," Shadow Hawk says. "Max Mayhem promised me he wouldn't harm her. And... I foolishly believed him."

"Why?" Meta-Man asks sternly. "Why would you trust him? Why would you trust my greatest enemy?"

"I was wrong to trust him with Susan's life," Shadow Hawk says. "But I wasn't wrong that you needed to be stopped."

"This time I'm going to destroy you once and for all," Meta-Man says. "And I'm going to enjoy every second of it."

"No, Meta-Man!" Warrior Woman says. "The Protectors of the Planet stick together. So, you're going to have to get through all of us first. Protectors, attack!"

Meta-Man's eyes go red and he fires a blast at Shadow Hawk who somersaults out of the way. Then, Goldrush is on Meta-Man first, hammering him with a series of high-speed blows, but he's not the hero he used to be and Meta-Man easily slaps him away with the back of his hand. The Marksman is next, unleashing a barrage of throwing stars that EXPLODE upon contact, catching Meta-Man by surprise. But Meta-Man quickly dispatches the former hero with a stomp to the ground, knocking the senior citizen easily off balance.

"Pick on someone your own strength!" Warrior

Woman says, running right at Meta-Man.

They grapple with one another, jostling for position, and to my surprise, Warrior Woman holds her own. But Meta-Man rolls backward, taking Warrior Woman with him, and then he lets go, flinging her into the sky.

"Warrior Woman!" Shadow Hawk yells.

But Meta-Man doesn't wait for a victory trophy, and instead charges at Shadow Hawk like a torpedo, pinning him to the ground.

"I'm going to enjoy this," Meta-Man says, his eyes crackling with bright, red energy.

"Shadow Hawk!" I yell. I've got to act fast, so I grab Goldrush's power and race over to stop Meta-Man. But a microsecond before I get there he raises his fist and I SLAM into it. I feel immense pain in my left side as he knocks the breath out of me and I careen into a rock wall!

He… did it again! Switched from… Heat Vision to… Super Speed to… Super Strength in… the blink of an eye. My left side feels like… it's on fire. I'm… so out of breath. Struggling for air.

But as I look back over, Meta-Man still has Shadow Hawk pinned. He can't get free! I… I don't know what to do. I… can barely stand… after that blow.

Then, Meta-Man's eyes light back up.

N-No! Got to… get up.

He'll… kill him.

But as I pull myself to my feet, I hear—

"Get off of him you monster!"

Out of the corner of my eye, I catch the downstroke of a metallic sword! Suddenly, a flash of red electricity escapes from Meta-Man's back. Meta-Man stands up and spins around, looking down with surprise as a thin line of electricity emanates from the 'MM' insignia on his chest. And then he looks up at me with terror in his eyes as the electricity rapidly expands, completely engulfing him in a giant, crackling ball of red light!

Suddenly, there's a blinding PFOOOM!

The force of the explosion blows me back against the rock and my side feels like it's on fire all over again. For a few seconds, all I see are stars. But as my vision clears, Meta-Man is gone, and Shadow Hawk is leaning over the body of a white-haired man in a hospital gown who is lying face down in the snow.

I-I can't believe it!

It's... the Black Crow!

And in his right hand is Max Mayhem Two's metallic sword. He... he saved Shadow Hawk's life! He destroyed Meta-Man!

BEEP! BEEP! BEEP!

W-What's that?

I look around but can't find the source of the noise. And then I realize it's coming from my utility belt. It's the Freedom Force transmitter Mom had TechnocRat put into my belt! I forgot all about it!

I push the button on the front and say, "H-Hello."

"Epic Z-ro?" comes Grace's broken voice, followed

by static. "Is th-t you?"

"Y-Yeah," I say.

"I- everyth--g okay?" she asks.

"Yeah," I say. "Everything... is just... dandy..."

"It -ook us for-ver to find -ou," she says. "What -re you doing at th- North P-le?"

But I can't answer.

Because the world goes black.

Meta Profile

Riptide

Name: Oceanus	Height: 6'0"
Race: Atlantean	Weight: 225 lbs
Status: Hero/Deceased	Eyes/Hair: Green/Green

META 3: Energy Manipulator	Observed Characteristics	
Extreme Water Manipulation	Combat 88	
Can Breathe on Land and Sea	Durability 90	Leadership 86
Wields Trident of Atlantis	Strategy 85	Willpower 94

EPILOGUE

I PUT IT ALL TOGETHER

"Elliott?" comes a familiar voice. "Are you okay?"

Who's calling me? I blink my eyes a few times and then open them to see a bunch of concerned faces looking down at me. I see Mom... and then... Dad. They're back! And on the other side is... Shadow Hawk!

"Y-You're okay!" I say, reaching out to him.

"I am," Shadow Hawk says, stepping forward and putting his hand on my shoulder. "And so are you, kid."

Then, I look around and see my all-too-familiar surroundings. "I'm in the Medi-wing again, aren't I?"

"We're thinking of renaming it the Epic-wing," Mom jokes with a smile. "You know, it would be great to come home and not find you here for once."

"Did you catch the Freaks of Nature?" I ask, trying to sit up. But then I feel a dull pain on my left side and look down to find my ribs wrapped in bandages.

"Easy, son," Dad says, helping to lower me back down. "You fractured three ribs. And yes, we caught the Freaks of Nature. It took a lot longer than we expected because they increased their ranks, but we got them all."

"That's great," I say, feeling my left side which is tender to the touch. No wonder I was in so much pain. Although I can't really remember how it happened.

"I filled everyone in while you were recovering," Shadow Hawk says. "I know they're proud of you for taking on Meta-Man."

Meta-Man! Suddenly, everything comes back to me. Meta-Man. Max Mayhem Two. The Protectors of the Planet. "The Black Crow!" I blurt out. "He used Max Mayhem's sword on Meta-Man. He saved us all. But is he...?"

"Yes, unfortunately," Shadow Hawk says, lowering his head. "That was his final act. Somehow, despite his deteriorating condition, he still had the strength to do what needed to be done. We all owe him our lives. I'll never know a greater man... or hero."

"I'm so sorry," I say.

"Thanks," Shadow Hawk says, looking me in the eyes. "But I owe you an apology. I should have told you I was Sparrow. I suppose I was trying to protect you, just like the Black Crow protected me. That's why I faked my own death at the nursing home. I knew if Meta-Man thought I was dead, he would leave you alone to kidnap the Black Crow. But I hurt you in the process and I'm deeply sorry for that."

"Hey, it's okay," I say. "I get it. Sometimes you do what you think is right to protect the people you care about. But I guess being honest is always better in the end. And that's how our team will always stay in harmony."

"You've got that right," Shadow Hawk says. "And you can count on me from here on out."

"What happened to the other Protectors?" I ask.

"The Marksman and Goldrush are okay," Shadow Hawk says. "And I found a very angry Warrior Woman a few miles away. She's the toughest lady I know. Unfortunately, Sergeant Stretch didn't make it. He was a great hero in his own right. I guess the only good to come out of this is that we're planning a real Protectors reunion to honor our friends who are no longer with us."

"Can I come with you?" I ask. "I'd like to thank them for everything they did, and it would be an honor to get to know them better."

"Of course," Shadow Hawk says, "and the honor would be all ours."

"Well, you do have some visitors here who have been waiting to see you," Mom says. "If you feel up for it?"

"My friends?" I ask. "They're here? Yes!"

"They waited all day," Dad says, opening the door.

"Come on in, guys. But remember, he's still recovering."

Suddenly, Dog-Gone and my friends come rushing through the door, followed by Grace. Dog-Gone reaches me first but Dad holds him back so he doesn't jump up on my bed.

"Whoa, boy," Dad says. "Take it easy. He's got ribs to heal."

I reach down to pet Dog-Gone who licks my hand.

"You wouldn't believe what he got into while you were gone," Grace says. "Let's just say we're out of jelly doughnuts... again."

"Oh, no," I say, looking at Dog-Gone.

"Not to mention disinfectant," Grace adds, rolling her eyes. "For the mess."

"I'm glad you're okay, Epic," Selfie says with a smile. "But don't ever run off like that again. Got it?"

I nod in agreement. Believe me, that was the last thing I wanted to do, but it was the only way I could get Max Mayhem Two to help us. I didn't know it would spiral out of control like that. And speaking of spiraling out of control, I still have to tell them that Max Mayhem Two was a clone—and there are at least ten others! But then I remember something else.

Terrog's ring!

It's still out there somewhere. I just hope we find it before Max Mayhem's clone does.

"Well, we'll give you some time to hang out with your friends," Dad says. "Besides, I'm heading to Lockdown to help TechnocRat repair the damage. And you know how irritable he'll get if I'm late."

"And I need to track down the escapees," Mom says.

That's right! Lockdown!

"How many villains got out?" I ask, dreading the answer. I only wish I could have stopped Meta-Man sooner.

"A lot," Mom says, "but don't worry about it now. You need to rest. We'll check in on you later."

Then, my parents exit.

"Are you guys hungry?" Shadow Hawk asks.

"Famished!" Pinball answers. Then, he looks at me and says, "Shadow Hawk promised to make us all cheeseburger funnel cakes. I'm finally gonna cash in!"

"That sounds gross," Skunk Girl says.

"Your loss," Pinball says. "More for me!"

"Would you like one, kid?" Shadow Hawk asks.

"Um, no thank you," I say. But then I get a sudden craving. "Shadow Hawk?"

"What's up?" he asks, stopping at the door.

"Well," I say, "I'd really love one of your peanut butter and banana sandwiches. You know, if that's okay?"

"You got it, kid," Shadow Hawk says with a wink. "I'm on the case."

"So, tell us about the whole Meta-Man mystery," Night Owl says to me. "What really happened out there?"

"Oh, it's a long story," I say, looking over at Shadow Hawk who is still standing at the door. I want to tell them everything, but I'm not really sure how he feels about me telling his story.

But then Shadow Hawk says, "He's right. It is a long story, but it's a good one. And it all started with Epic Zero figuring out that I was Sparrow. Isn't that right, Epic Zero?"

"Yeah," I say with a smile. "That's right."

"Then you should tell them everything," he says. "And don't leave out any of the good parts. I'll be right back with your food." And then he winks again and exits.

As Shadow Hawk leaves I smile.

And then I tell the team everything.

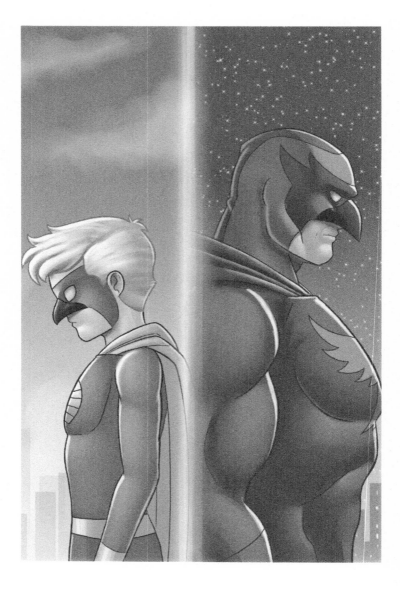

YOU CAN MAKE A BIG DIFFERENCE

Calling all heroes! I need your help to get Epic Zero 8 in front of more readers.

Reviews are extremely helpful in getting attention for my books. I wish I had the marketing muscle of the major publishers, but instead, I have something far more valuable, loyal readers, just like you! Your generosity in providing an honest review will help bring this book to the attention of more readers.

So, if you've enjoyed this book, I would be very grateful if you could spare a minute to leave a review on the book's Amazon page. Thanks for your support!

Stay Epic!

R.L. Ullman

META POWERS GLOSSARY

FROM THE META MONITOR:

There are nine known Meta power classifications. These classifications have been established to simplify Meta identification and provide a quick framework to understand a Meta's potential powers and capabilities. **Note:** Metas can possess powers in more than one classification. In addition, Metas can evolve over time in both the powers they express, as well as the effectiveness of their powers.

Due to the wide range of Meta abilities, superpowers have been further segmented into power levels. Power levels differ across Meta power classifications. In general, the following power levels have been established:

- Meta 0: Displays no Meta power.
- Meta 1: Displays limited Meta power.
- Meta 2: Displays considerable Meta power.
- Meta 3: Displays extreme Meta power.

The following is a brief overview of the nine Meta power classifications.

ENERGY MANIPULATION:

Energy Manipulation is the ability to generate, shape, or act as a conduit, for various forms of energy. Energy Manipulators can control energy by focusing or redirecting energy towards a specific target or shaping/reshaping energy for a specific task. Energy Manipulators are often impervious to the forms of energy they can manipulate.

Examples of the types of energies utilized by Energy Manipulators include, but are not limited to:

- Atomic
- Chemical
- Cosmic
- Electricity
- Gravity
- Heat
- Light
- Magnetic
- Sound
- Space
- Time

Note: the fundamental difference between an Energy Manipulator and a Meta-morph with Energy Manipulation capability is that an Energy Manipulator does not change their physical, molecular state to either generate or transfer energy (see META-MORPH).

FLIGHT:
Flight is the ability to fly, glide, or levitate above the Earth's surface without the use of an external source (e.g. jetpack). Flight can be accomplished through a variety of methods, these include, but are not limited to:

- Reversing the forces of gravity
- Riding air currents
- Using planetary magnetic fields
- Wings

Metas exhibiting Flight can range from barely sustaining flight a few feet off the ground to reaching the far limits of outer space.

Often, Metas with Flight ability also display the complementary ability of Super-Speed. However, it can be difficult to decipher if Super-Speed is a Meta power in its own right or is simply a function of combining the Meta's Flight ability with the Earth's natural gravitational force.

MAGIC:
Magic is the ability to display a wide variety of Meta abilities by channeling the powers of a secondary magical or mystical source. Known secondary sources of Magic powers include, but are not limited to:

- Alien lifeforms
- Dark arts
- Demonic forces
- Departed souls
- Mystical spirits

Typically, the forces of Magic are channeled through an enchanted object. Known magical, enchanted objects include:

- Amulets
- Books
- Cloaks
- Gemstones
- Wands

- Weapons

Some Magicians can transport themselves into the mystical realm of their magical source. They may also have the ability to transport others into and out of these realms as well.

Note: the fundamental difference between a Magician and an Energy Manipulator is that a Magician typically channels their powers from a mystical source that likely requires the use of an enchanted object to express these powers (see ENERGY MANIPULATOR).

META MANIPULATION:
Meta Manipulation is the ability to duplicate or negate the Meta powers of others. Meta Manipulation is a rare Meta power and can be extremely dangerous if the Meta Manipulator is capable of manipulating the powers of multiple Metas at one time. Meta Manipulators who can manipulate the powers of several Metas at once have been observed to reach Meta 4 power levels.

Based on the unique powers of the Meta Manipulator, it is hypothesized that other abilities could include altering or controlling the powers of others. Despite their tremendous abilities, Meta Manipulators are often unable to generate powers of their own and are limited to manipulating the powers of others. When not utilizing their abilities, Meta Manipulators may be vulnerable to attack.

Note: It has been observed that a Meta Manipulator requires close physical proximity to a Meta target to fully manipulate their power. When fighting a Meta

Manipulator, it is advised to stay at a reasonable distance and to attack from long range. Meta Manipulators have been observed manipulating the powers of others up to 100 yards away.

META-MORPH:

Meta-morph is the ability to display a wide variety of Meta abilities by "morphing" all, or part, of one's physical form from one state into another. There are two sub-types of Meta-morphs:

- Physical
- Molecular

Physical morphing occurs when a Meta-morph transforms their physical state to express their powers. Physical Meta-morphs typically maintain their human physiology while exhibiting their powers (with the exception of Shapeshifters). Types of Physical morphing include, but are not limited to:

- Invisibility
- Malleability (elasticity/plasticity)
- Physical by-products (silk, toxins, etc…)
- Shapeshifting
- Size changes (larger or smaller)

Molecular morphing occurs when a Meta-morph transforms their molecular state from a normal physical state to a non-physical state to express their powers. Types of Molecular morphing include, but are not limited to:

- Fire
- Ice
- Rock
- Sand
- Steel
- Water

Note: Because Meta-morphs can display abilities that mimic all other Meta power classifications, it can be difficult to properly identify a Meta-morph upon the first encounter. However, it is critical to carefully observe how their powers manifest, and, if it is through Physical or Molecular morphing, you can be certain you are dealing with a Meta-morph.

PSYCHIC:
Psychic is the ability to use one's mind as a weapon. There are two sub-types of Psychics:

- Telepaths
- Telekinetics

Telepathy is the ability to read and influence the thoughts of others. While Telepaths often do not appear to be physically intimidating, their power to penetrate minds can often result in more devastating damage than a physical assault.

Telekinesis is the ability to manipulate physical objects with one's mind. Telekinetics can often move objects with their mind that are much heavier than they could move physically. Many Telekinetics can also make objects move at very high speeds.

Note: Psychics are known to strike from long distance, and, in a fight, it is advised to incapacitate them as quickly as possible. Psychics often become physically drained from the extended use of their powers.

SUPER-INTELLIGENCE:
Super-Intelligence is the ability to display levels of intelligence above standard genius intellect. Super-Intelligence can manifest in many forms, including, but not limited to:

- Superior analytical ability
- Superior information synthesizing
- Superior learning capacity
- Superior reasoning skills

Note: Super-Intellects continuously push the envelope in the fields of technology, engineering, and weapons development. Super-Intellects are known to invent new approaches to accomplish previously impossible tasks. When dealing with a Super-Intellect, you should be mentally prepared to face challenges that have never been encountered before. In addition, Super-Intellects can come in all shapes and sizes. The most advanced Super-Intellects have originated from non-human creatures.

SUPER-SPEED:
Super-Speed is the ability to display movement at remarkable physical speeds above standard levels of speed. Metas with Super-Speed often exhibit complementary abilities to movement that include, but are not limited to:

- Enhanced endurance
- Phasing through solid objects
- Super-fast reflexes
- Time travel

Note: Metas with Super-Speed often have an equally super metabolism, burning thousands of calories per minute, and requiring them to eat many extra meals a day to maintain consistent energy levels. It has been observed that Metas exhibiting Super-Speed are quick thinkers, making it difficult to keep up with their thought process.

SUPER-STRENGTH:

Super-Strength is the ability to utilize muscles to display remarkable levels of physical strength above expected levels of strength. Metas with Super-Strength can lift or push objects that are well beyond the capability of an average member of their species. Metas exhibiting Super-Strength can range from lifting objects twice their weight to incalculable levels of strength allowing for the movement of planets.

Metas with Super-Strength often exhibit complementary abilities to strength that include, but are not limited to:

- Earthquake generation through stomping
- Enhanced jumping
- Invulnerability
- Shockwave generation through clapping

Note: Metas with Super-Strength may not always possess this strength evenly. Metas with Super-Strength have been observed to demonstrate powers in only one arm or leg.

META PROFILE CHARACTERISTICS

FROM THE META MONITOR:

In addition to having a strong working knowledge of a Meta's powers and capabilities, it is also imperative to understand the key characteristics that form the core of their character. When facing or teaming up with Metas, understanding their key characteristics will help you gain deeper insight into their mentality and strategic potential.

What follows is a brief explanation of the five key characteristics you should become familiar with. **Note:** the data that appears in each Meta profile has been compiled from live field activity.

COMBAT:

The ability to defeat a foe in hand-to-hand combat.

DURABILITY:

The ability to withstand significant wear, pressure, or damage.

LEADERSHIP:

The ability to lead a team of disparate personalities and powers to victory.

STRATEGY:

The ability to find, and successfully exploit, a foe's weakness.

WILLPOWER:

The ability to persevere, despite seemingly insurmountable odds.

ABOUT THE AUTHOR

R.L. Ullman is the bestselling author of the award-winning EPIC ZERO series and the award-winning MONSTER PROBLEMS series. He creates fun, engaging page-turners that captivate the imaginations of kids and adults alike. His original, relatable characters face adventure and adversity that bring out their inner strengths. He's frequently distracted thinking up new stories, and once got lost in his own neighborhood. You can learn more about what R.L. is up to at rlullman.com, and if you see him wandering around your street please point him in the right direction home.

ACKNOWLEDGMENTS

Without the support of these brave heroes, I would have been trampled by supervillains before I could bring this series to print. I would like to thank my wife, Lynn (a.k.a. Mrs. Marvelous); my son Matthew (a.k.a. Captain Creativity); my daughter Olivia (a.k.a. Ms. Positivity); and my furry sidekicks Howie and Sadie. I would also like to thank all of the readers out there who have connected with Elliott and his amazing family. Stay Epic!